Freaky

by Emilia di Girolamo

emilia di girolamo

First published London, 1999 by Spacehopper

(Spacehopper is an imprint and trading name of Pulp Faction Ltd)

e-mail spacehopper@pulpfact.demon.co.uk

Spacehopper, PO Box 12171, London N19 3HB

©1999 Emilia di Girolamo

ISBN 1901072 150

Author photograph Merrilees Brown
Cover design by BigCorporateDisco
Printed in England by Cox and Wyman

freaky

A very special thank you to: Mick Thorne.

The author would also like to thank: Dom Chapman, Max Kempster, Paul Marsh, Barry Fantoni, Stephen Plaice, Anna Reynolds, Cav. Romeo & Megan di Girolamo, Max Allen, Jarvis Cocker, Jo Carter, Ruth Thompsett, Charlotte Conquest, Selina & Mike, Jemima, Daniel Barzotti, Johnny Mario, Scope, Chunky NC, Jamie 'Torch Boy' Page, Charlotte Bellamy, Mungo Denison, Starsky, Gavin Forward, Stephen Flannigan, Margi Riley, Colin Macnamara, Louis Hyde, Danny Hubbard, Catherine Glasser, Naomi Glasser, Vincent Mitchell, Skag, Alan Lacroix, Robert Afflick, Simon at Plastic Head, Trevor Holden, Pulp, The Addicts, Elaine Palmer and all at Spacehopper.

This book is dedicated to Dom Chapman for his love support and inspiration

Contents

'Now listen; these freaks we're talking about, they're just normal people gone a bit wrong that's all. Something happened to them and they never got over it. Now they walk around in a daze with twisted innards and blank faces, wanting to join in but too scared to make the jump. It's sad but don't bother crying; they still eat and drink and watch TV just like anyone else. And they smoke.'

(from album sleeve of **'FREAKS'** by **PULP**)

1. Death Flies

It was the day my Grandfather died that I first heard about Clemente's condition. 'Is Aunty Joanna coming over?' I asked my mother through our brittle silence. 'No, she isn't,' she answered rubbing her eyes with a bundle of loo roll, 'she has to stay and look after Clemmi.'

I wanted to ask my mother 'Why?' but with her father lying there dead and everything, well, it didn't seem right. Instead I said, 'D'you want some tea? I'll get you some shall I?' and I headed off to the green walled canteen in order to give my mother some time alone. Also, I suppose, I wanted to avoid that family/death/huggy/tears thing.

The tears were quite involuntary in the first place, and not even nearly intended or indeed imagined, (and believe me I knew it was coming, we all did). But death kind of does that to me. I know you'd expect that from most people but you don't really know me yet and when you do you'll understand pretty much. You'll see why crying and shit like that doesn't come easy to me.

I sat in the hospital canteen by a dying cheese plant trying to control my emotions and drinking tepid black coffee. It had that nasty aftertaste you get with instant supermarket own brands. I'm funny about coffee, I like it black and strong and real. Couldn't live without my cafetière. Can't stand the instant stuff and I never did believe the hype. Never did swallow the adverts.

I sipped at the coffee and floating kettle scale with its designer flavour, 'eau d' disinfectant,' bought my mother a cup of tea, and headed back to the death watch ways of the ward.

Mum was crying and dabbing her nose with the now soaking tissues. She was holding Grandpa's icy hands with their paper thin skin, and muttering to herself.

'I brought tea,' I said, 'and a Kit Kat.' My palms were sweaty and I could feel the chocolate melting in my clenched hand.

'Thanks, love,' she said sniffing. She turned to me then, lifting her head dreadfully slowly and looking at me with questioning eyes, 'He was a good man really. He was.' It wasn't me she was trying to convince and I wondered about the untold secrets of her childhood.

She placed his hands back where they came from, underneath the tight white sheets, gulped the tea and sighed loudly. I watched the motion of her mouth and listened to the sound of her swallowing in the silence of the ward.

She didn't say anything for ages and then out of the brittle air came her thick voice, 'Well, better get back to the house and start making phone calls.'

'Shall I talk to the nurse about arrangements?' I asked quickly.

'No it's alright love, it's all done. They're taking him to the mortuary. They have to do an autopsy,' she said, the tears starting up again, 'to determine exactly what caused his death.'

'Don't they know?' I asked confused. Grandpa had been in the hospital for over six weeks, feebly clinging to life's last threads.

'Well they have to be sure.'

'What about the undertakers? Shouldn't we call them now?' I asked, feeling it was too quick to leave.

'Lilly is arranging all that,' Mum said mopping her eyes.

'I ought to see her before we leave,' I said realising I had barely spoken to my step Grandmother.

'She's gone home love, she's terribly upset. Her sister's with her.' With those words Mum rose from her chair, brushed the crumbs of wafer and chocolate from her tweeded lap, picked up her bag and left the ward with a click of high heels. I smelt her perfume as she passed and it stank of death and vanilla.

I followed her quickly, fumbling for the car keys in my rucksack and finding six packets of Rizlas, four lighters, a travelcard and a squashed lipstick, *Damson Distress* I think but the label was covered in mascara so it was hard to tell for sure.

I drove in silence and Mum sat with her face turned towards the window, her chin buried in the soft neck of her fake angora jumper. I guessed she was probably crying but if she was she did so without a sound and without turning my way once. It was a long drive back to Tring from Birmingham, with the Friday traffic. The M6 is always a complete nightmare on a Friday.

I thought about a lot of things on that journey. I thought about Grandpa and what it was like when I was a child. I recalled his crazy stories, holidays in his caravan when Granny was still alive. I thought about the swimming medal he gave me when I was twelve when I did my Bronze at school. He taught me to swim my Grandpa. Every Sunday morning we walked to the baths with fat towels, just the two of us. He'd stand on the side and shout instructions. Taught me the breast stroke first, then the crawl and when I was eleven he taught me the butterfly and I felt so grown up. After swimming he'd take me to a café where we'd eat soggy Cornish pasties and drink fizzy orange. He always kept a Caramac bar for me to find in the glove compartment of his car.

He told me about the war. I asked him if he'd ever killed a man and he had tears in his eyes when he answered me. He was English though his hair and skin were dark. He had sparkly blue eyes always full of smiles.

Stuck in traffic and in our silence I touched Mum's hand gently, 'Are you alright?' I asked.

'I'm fine,' Mum said, 'it's just all so sad. There's no-one left now is there? It's just me and your Dad. No-one to visit at the weekends.'

I didn't know what to say. I wanted to make her pain disappear but I couldn't even take away the smallest part of it.

'Maybe you should persuade Joanna to come over from Italy,' I suggested, 'you need her now.'

'I told you she can't, not with Clemmi unwell. Anyway you know what she's like. They've never got any money,' Mum sounded angry when she talked about her sister and I wasn't surprised. Joanna had known Grandpa was dying but she had barely made the effort to call let alone come and see him.

'What's wrong with Clemmi?' I asked then, concerned about my favourite cousin, 'Is she ill?'

'I don't know exactly. Joanna said she's had some sort of a breakdown,' Mum said vaguely. I didn't push it. I knew that mental illness was one of those subjects reserved for hushed voices and scant details in our family.

My aunt Joanna is married to my Dad's brother Claudio. That's the way they like it in Sicily. Two brothers married to two sisters, a perfect match. It could only be more perfect if Mum and Joanna were Italian. In the old days the cousins would then marry, hence the numerous cases of inbreeding on the island. Grandpa Wilson never approved. I think he wanted nice English husbands for his daughters rather than a couple of 'Iti's' as he used to call them. At Christmas when Clemmi and I were kids, we would leave the room during the Queen's speech claiming we were Italian and she wasn't our Queen. Grandpa would get really angry at us; 'You should be proud to be British,' he used to say. We used to giggle and sing the Italian national anthem so we didn't have to listen to his nationalistic rant.

As children Clemmi and I were inseparable. Then Joanna and Claudio moved to Italy and we relied on summer holidays and letters to maintain our bond.

After Granny died, Grandpa re-married and Clemmi stopped visiting him. I stopped too. I suppose I never forgave him for soiling Granny's memory by loving someone else. Grandpa and his new wife Lilly moved to Birmingham and we drifted apart. I never made the effort because I couldn't see him as the same person. I regret it now. We were so close once. I suppose I loved him.

I have to say it was a relief when I dropped Mother off outside the red brick house and said, 'Say hi to Dad, yeah? And call me, about the... the funeral and that.'

'Of course I will,' she said sharply, 'yes, of course.' I thought I'd got away with it but no such luck.

'Aren't you coming in then?' she gave me that look, the one that made me feel I was a big disappointment to her.

'I don't know ... there's stuff I've got to do and...'

Well I tried.

'I don't believe you sometimes, what's your father going to say? At least come in for a cup of coffee.'

'Right,' I said turning the ignition off.

Great, just what I needed, another big Sicilian lecture on family and duty and what a useless daughter I was.

I picked up my bag and opened the car door. Mum walked towards the house her heels catching in the gravel and I have to say I pitied her. She looked tired and old. I'd never seen her like that before. I followed her up the path and into the red brick semi to find Dad slouched on the burgundy draylon sofa, cigar in mouth, watching Italian football.

'Hi Dad,' I said trying to smile a bit.

'What youa bloody want then?' That was his way of greeting me.

Mum went straight to the kitchen and put the kettle on.

'Totò,' she called, 'do you want expresso?'

Dad grunted. I wanted to have a go at him. I mean Mum had just been to say goodbye to her dead father and he didn't even ask how she was.

'Totò?' Mum called again.

'That's a yes Mum,' I shouted back. I decided to try to hold my anger back for Mum's sake and make conversation.

'Are Napoli winning then?' I asked gesturing to the screen.

'No they nota bloody winning! Theya bloody useless!'

Typical Italian: love your team when they're winning, hate them when they're losing.

'Juve were good last night, did you see it?'

Grunt.

I tried again, 'They'll be better once Del Piero's ankle's fixed up. They need him don't you think?'

'What-a the 'ell d'you a know about foot-a-ball? You are a bloody girl!' Dad said laughing and spluttering on his cigar, tiny flecks of saliva clinging to his thick moustache. I have to say he pissed me off with that comment 'cause if there's one thing I know about it's Italian football.

I decided to change the subject.

'How's Zia Ornella?' I asked, trying to show some interest in the family.

'No too bad. Your cugina Gelsomina is marrying a lovely man, very rich, 'e gotta 'is own company car. The family come from Palermo, very good family, they got alotta money.'

'That's nice,' I said, 'send Gelsomina my love when you see her.'

''Ow can I senda your love to Gelsomina? I can't a bloody mention your name in that 'ouse can I? My poor *sorella*! *Disgraziata*! You shame all of us! Gelsomina is four years younger thana you and already she got 'erself a nice man. Who bloody wanna marry you *svergognata*?'

'That's alright Dad,' I said, 'I don't want to get married.'

Mum came in with the coffee. 'You two talking about Gelsomina's wedding?'

'Yes,' I said. 'Dad was telling me about all the wonderful qualities her fiancé has, weren't you Dad?'

Mum handed me an expresso and I knocked it back quickly.

'Totò did you tell her about the cake Gels is having? Ooh it's going to have ten tiers! Ten, can you believe it?' Mum's eyes were wide and she seemed to have cheered up a bit.

'Ten? Wow!' I said, 'Why's that then? Did the last Italian wedding in Aylesbury have nine?'

Mum ignored my sarcasm, '...and the dress, Totò did you tell her? The train is ten feet long and the dress is all oyster silk, just like Princess Di's, God bless her soul, with little jewels all over it. Lorenzo and Ornella paid two thousand pounds for it! Two thousand!' Even Mum was beginning to sound Italian.

'That's good,' I said. 'Gelsomina will be able to pawn it when her husband has gambled the house keeping away!'

'That isn't very kind is it?' Mum said.

'Well he's Sicilian isn't he?' I snapped back looking at Dad.

'I expect you are just jealous of your cousin. I don't hear any wedding bells ringing for you young lady!'

Mum placed her cup carefully back on the tray.

'If you two think I'm going to marry some stupid Sicilian and spend my life chained to a kitchen sink with six kids and another one for a husband then you're sadly mistaken! I didn't go to college to spend my life washing dishes and cooking 'sagna.'

Dad looked at me like I was nothing, 'That's just as bloody well. No decent Sicilian boy woulda touch you. Not with your record.'

'I'm twenty five Dad, I can do what I want and I don't want to get married, not to anyone and definitely not some dumb Sicilian factory boy!'

Dad turned to me slowly and spoke in one of his particularly dramatic mafia movie ways, 'What a beautiful carnation you turned out to be.'

I wanted to laugh because Dad's poignant saying lost a lot in translation. 'I have to go,' I said standing quickly, 'take care then.'

'Oh yes, youa bloody rusha back to London, don't you care about your poor Mamma,' Dad shouted. I ignored him.

'See you Mum, look after yourself alright?'

'Yes love and you, drive carefully,' she said walking to the door with me.

I got into the car hoping to God I'd get it started.

'Well take care then, I'll see you really soon, okay?' I said, trying to sound cheerful. She leaned across to me then and offered me a cold cheek through the car window. I kissed it uncertainly, wishing for something more.

By some miracle the car started first time and I swung round in a U-turn and headed off towards the motorway. I stopped for petrol at the garage just past the Chinese. I was off in a dreamworld, waiting for the pump to click off, watching the numbers drift by, inhaling the fumes as the petrol poured into my faded red Triumph Herald 1360 convertible.

God I love the smell of petrol. Always did. Used to open the back window of the car and sniff it when I was a kid, until Dad would notice and say, 'Stop it, it's notta bloody good for you.' That just made me like it all the more. I couldn't wait to grow old enough to get my own car and inhale petrol fumes just as much as I liked. I rummaged for coins to make up the balance and asked for some Rizlas when I got the change, feeling pretty shit remembering the six packets in my bag as he handed them to me. Oh well, you can never have enough Rizlas can you? That's what my mate Sasha says.

As I started to make my way back on to the A41, a blue Fiat Panda soft top with an improvised coat hanger aerial, dented wing and miniature Spurs kit hanging from the rear view mirror whizzed by and I knew instantly it was Jimmi's car. I felt my palms sticky with sweat against the vinyl steering wheel.

My hands were hot with sweat the night I left him too. We were

sitting in the squat, everyone too stoned to move as usual, Jimmi
dreaming up London, dreaming up twenty-four hour clubland
and coffeebars with funky music and good looking chicks.

'And we'll get a place. Us two and you guys if you're in?'

'Too right, Jimmi, we're in man.'

'Yeah,' I said, 'Not more than fifteen minutes from the centre.'

'Yeah, and we'll get an extra room so we can do a dope factory.
And a cat eh Sash, like Skag, we'll get a ginger tom like Skaggy.'

'I'd rather live in Brighton thanks Zig, fuck London.'

'Listen Ziggy, no fucking cats man, we gotta sort us first.'
Johnny intervened putting his can down hard to make his point.
(A whole lot of people thought Ziggy must be really into Bowie
to end up with a name like that, truth is it aint got nish to do with
Bowie. No, we call Ziggy Ziggy 'cause of Quantum Leap.)

'I want a cat man, come on Johnny, this place aint been the
same since the R.T.A.'

'Don't be so melodramatic Ziggy, it was only a fucking cat
man!' Johnny said, rubbing his freshly shaved head.

'It was Skag, Johnny, it was Skag.'

I was skinning up so I avoided the cat argument. There was
something different to argue about every day; the guy that ripped
Johnny off with a gram of coke that was mostly glucose, whose
turn it was to buy bog roll, who'd been pruning the hemp plant

on the stairwell, the price of a good bit of hydroponic skunk. Too many arguments. The big escape plan just made it worse. Ziggy wanted a cat and to live in Islington because he loved angels. Jimmi fancied Camden 'because of the vibe man, and you can always get a new T-shirt on a Sunday.' Bo fancied Portobello because he'd read too much Martin Amis and Sasha wanted to live in Wood Green because she knew a good dealer there. I wanted to live any place we could get that was cheap enough.

Anyway, I'd had it with them bickering about the cat stuff, I stood up and said, 'Right. I'm going now, who's coming?'

I waited for an answer.

'I thought you were skinning up Jay,' Sasha said, tugging at the blonde tangles of her hair as she lolled back on the sofa.

'We smoked it Sash, while the boys were talking Sheba or Felix,' I said, picking up my tobacco from the coffee stained table.

'Oh yeah,' Sasha said, sliding her feet across the table to reach for the communal skunk with her toes.

'I mean it guys, I'm goin' tonight. On the last train.' I waited for them to jump up and say, I'm with you Jay. But they didn't. Sasha was too busy looking for some more spliff and Johnny and Ziggy were discussing the cost of neutering cats and the ethics of the issue and Bo was talking to the wallpaper; I guessed he'd taken those Strawberries Uncle Bob gave us as a taster last Tuesday.

'I'm out of here guys,' I shouted above the Doors track we'd heard fourteen times as Jimmi had clicked the repeat button in his stoned state. 'I'll wait for you to pack if you're coming,' I said.

I tried again, 'Jimmi? Come on, we can all pile in the Panda.' But deep down I knew none of them would, not even Jimmi.

So I ended up leaving Tring with a final image of Jimmi, Bo, Johnny, Ziggy and Sasha sitting around the squat out of their heads. Jimmi didn't even try to stop me. The last words I heard as I went down the stairs were,

'I loved that cat Johnny, you'll never know how much.'

'Zig, man, pass the Rizlas, I aint got no roach left here man.'

'It was just a fucking cat, what about life man, human life. Haven't you ever lost someone close?'

'Yeah, my mother died when I was thirteen.'

'Oh shit man, Zig babe, I didn't know that man, I wouldn't have said it yeah. We'll get a cat Zig, we'll get two.'

I slammed the door. Half to make a point and half because I hoped they'd stop me. I mean Jimmi was my boyfriend, those were my mates, how could they let me face the big shitty on my own? But they did.

When I got to Euston I didn't have a clue where to go, so I got a tube on the light blue line and kipped down in a shop doorway just off Oxford Street. Back entrance to HMV I think it was. It was the only place I really knew of, Oxford Street. I mean I recognised High Street Kensington and Camden because I'd been to the markets, and Euston because I'd been up to Manchester on the train when Jimmi's car was fucked and we had a party to go to. And I knew Hampstead where my cousin Fabrizio lived. But I didn't have a clue about Highbury and Brixton or Finsbury Park or Old Street. I thought Oxford Circus sounded fun and I knew there were lots of shops, well compared to Tring that is. I mean Tring's so slow, two takeaways, The King's Arms, Cancer Dave's house on a Friday night and a museum. Jesus, how could I have found that place interesting? I suppose anything would be exciting after Bovingdon, where my parents lived. The car boot sale was the highlight of my week.

I was sharing my doorway with a load of soggy boxes and a cardboard cut out of Rick Astley! It was getting chilly being September and I only had my bag for a pillow and a light duvet, grabbed from our bed as an afterthought and to piss Jimmi off. I settled in the door way feeling insulted when a woman with dyed black matted hair, stiletto boots and a Marilyn Manson T-shirt tossed me twenty pence and a half smoked B&H. I gave them to Rick and settled down for the night.

It didn't take long to find a more permanent residence. I got chatting to some geezer in a pub in Old Street and before I knew it me and my rucksack had moved into a squat in Holloway.

Within three months I was flat sharing in Crouch End courtesy of housing benefit and a few hours bar work cash in hand. I've moved around a lot since then, Hornsey, Camden, Wood Green, Tufnell Park, always staying north of the river as if I couldn't quite let go of the M1, my route back to Jimmi and the others.

2. Feeling Myself Again

I sit at the bar in The Maynard, pub from hell but one of my old locals from my Crouch End days. It's one of those pubs that used to be really wicked but got taken over by some naff chain. It's got shitloads of fishing nets and lobster pots stuck to the ceiling and a big carp in a glass case. A nautical theme pub (like Crouch End is anywhere near the sea!) They even have this guy (called God on account of his long white hair and incredibly overgrown white beard) who goes round the pub on a Friday night selling bright pink fish sticks and little pots of cockles and mussels served up on polystyrene trays, drowned in vinegar and thousand island dressing. People sometimes clap and make seal noises when he comes in; it depends how fishy they're feeling.

  Usually I grab my favourite seat if it's free and I'm with my mates. It's right opposite the gents so I get to survey every man in the pub. That way I also get the chance to give my prey a long lingering look if necessary, like if he's fit and I fancy a shag or something. Anyway, tonight I'm on my own so I sit at the bar and wait for someone interesting to come in. I'm drinking vodka and tonic and smoking Merit cigarettes. My mate brought them back from Italy for me, knowing I've got a bit of a thing about them. I slide off the bar stool and walk through the crowded pub, past the blackboard offering *Krazy Steaks*,

(Hang on a minute, three points:

1: Why the K?

2: What's Krazy about them anyway?

3: The only thing it makes me think of is mad cow disease and that don't do nish for my appetite.)

The jukebox is playing Scope's 'Song For Bobby': I slink past it towards the toilet, counting the admiring glances and surveying the lads for a suitable shag. I check my appearance in the cracked mirror and push the doors to find a free cubicle. The seat's broken so I choose another, kneel down and empty the paltry contents of a wrap on the seat. I cut it as quickly as I can and snort with my left nostril because my right one's still scabby from the weekend. I lick the wrap, get anaesthetic tongue and sniff hard. I flush the loo and sit on the seat for a second wishing I'd blown my nose first. I start reading the graffiti on the toilet wall, smudgy lipstick and black marker pen. *'I shagged Callum Mc Neil!'* and then a long list of *'Me too!'* and *'So did* I' followed by, *'Fuck off bitches, he's mine.'* Girls can be so stupid. Mind you, I have to say, he was good. He had this massive iron bed with tight white cotton sheets and a pair of handcuffs permanently fixed to the bedstead. Good looking too, blond curly hair and a tan all the way from Ibiza. He found me in Florian's looking for action and on account of his reputation I made him work for it. He gave me a wrap of coke on my birthday, stuck his tongue in my ear and said, *'Don't say I never give you nothing!'* He was sweet like that and he knew how to have a good time. He certainly gave me one.

I have a piss, check my appearance again, fluff up my hair and head back to my vodka. Some guy's nicked my stool but that's alright because he's drop dead so I just slide in next to him and retrieve my cigarettes and drink.

'Sorry, did I take your seat?' he says.

'Yeah but it's cool, I'm fine standing,' I say, smiling my best pulling smile and giving him a little wink.

'You sure?' he says.

'Yeah,' I say swallowing the ice cubes at the bottom of my glass.

'Fancy another drink?' Blondie says. I call him that 'cause his hair's bleached.

'Ta, vodka and tonic please.'

Oh how I love men with bleached hair—they have the strangest effect on me.

Blondie orders the drinks and I notice he's drinking Pernod with water. Kind of a strange drink really. Not many guys drink Pernod. I mean in the eighties yeah, with blackcurrant but not these days and definitely not guys. He gets up then and returns with a stool for me.

'Cheers,' I say.

'I'm Vinnie,' he says, 'what's your name?'

I make one up: 'Chrissy.'

'Good to make your acquaintance Chrissy,' he says holding out his hand to me. I squeeze it lightly and look directly into his eyes. He holds my gaze and I like what I'm getting.

'Do you live round here?' I ask.

'Yeah, not far, Topsfield Parade, above '*Chunky Nice Clothing*' he says swallowing his Pernod and clicking the ice in his mouth.

'Alone?' I ask.

'Yes, alone,' he replies cautiously.

I notice that his eyes are the deepest blue.

'Come on then,' I say, slipping my jacket on.

Blondie looks kind of non-plussed then but follows me out of the pub anyway. His flat is warm which is a bonus really. He offers me coffee and goes to the kitchen. I listen to the kettle boiling and slip out of my clothes. When he comes back into the room to ask if I take sugar he nearly drops the coffee.

I walk across to him and start undoing his fly with my teeth. He lets out a little gasp and I know I've got him. His hips are slim and boyish and I like that. I take a long slow swallow of hot coffee, swishing it around my mouth, then I go down on him and give him the best head he ever had in his life. When he's come he collapses on the green velvet sofa, and says,

'Chrissy that was great!'

'Yeah?' I say, acting a bit coy.

'Yeah!' he says beckoning for me to sit beside him.

I ignore his request and get dressed. He doesn't say anything. Gets up once to put a CD on and sits down again. My mate D-Chunk says you can tell a whole lot about someone's personality from their CD collection, but he's a DJ and I don't have time for analysis. The track comes on while I'm lacing up my trainers. It's something or other by Arab Strap and I like it. I cross the room, sit astride him and give him a long hard kiss. As I pull away I say,

'See ya,' and cross the room to the door.

'Can I have your number?' he says his pretty blue eyes wide and confused.

'Sure,' I say, noticing the pen and pad by the phone. I write, 'Chrissy—0898 696969' blow him a kiss and leave fast. Well, I've got things to do. I've got people to see and an engagement party to get to.

3. Club Revenge

I stand with my back to the wall and count the pairs of Nike trainers shuffling ahead of me wishing I wasn't freezing my tits off in Brixton at just before midnight. But I know this is where I will find Mr K and the likelihood of getting a couple of grams on credit. The queue shuffles a few inches and a girl with blue and green dreadlocks asks me for a light. I spark up the silver lighter that my mate Jamie bought me last week after a night of clubbing and a morning of bitter expresso and Italian football at Bar Italia.

'God we've been out here for ages Stace,' says the girl with the multicoloured dreads.

'Shut ya whinging, I told ya it's werf it! Wicked sounds man,' is the retort from her equally multicoloured friend, zipping her mock seventies retro ski jacket up tighter against the cold drizzle.

Stace turns to me then, 'You on yer own?'

I can't resist mimicking her drugged up South London accent, mostly put on I'm sure. 'Na,' I reply, 'meeting me mates inside, they're like DJs you know.'

'No really? Wick-ed man! Like you know the DJs?' she comes back at me sounding depressingly impressed.

'Yep,' I say sniffing like I've just done shitloads of coke, 'known 'em for years.'

'Wow!' she says.

'Should've been on the guestlist and that but Squeamish fucked up, my name aint on it, otherwise I'd get you in quick like, none of this queuing and shit,' I say, trying to sound like I'm something.

'Oh that's 'kay,' Stace says quickly, 'it's all part of the fun innit?' Her friend throws her a look of surprise, probably recalling her moaning.

The crowd surges forward suddenly and I guess the clock just struck twelve and the 'half price before midnight' deal just wore off. Someone pushes me from behind and shoves me into Stace and her too cool mate. 'Watch it,' I say turning round, fists ready. 'Sorry luv,' says the accused's mate, 'he's out of it.' I relinquish my aggression reluctantly and head for the doors. Stace and her uptight mate have disappeared inside so I suppose that's something.

I have to get one thing straight, right from the start, I'm not Miss Club Queen, no way. I mean, I'm here for a reason. I'm not saying I don't like clubs, I do, but not this kind. I've done all that stuff and most of the kids here, like Stace for example, are practically half my age. I mean there's certain parties I never miss like F.L.Y. and Subvert. You get a decent crowd there, older, and the sounds aren't trance and techno shit like this place. No. I'm on a mission tonight and it's not about the drugs, they just help me along a bit.

The club is buzzing, it's fucking packed. The DJ's doing his worst and the dancefloor's heaving. Girls with bindis and glow in the dark jewellery dance stupidly, hands weaving above their heads. A tall bloke with no shirt on is making boxes with his hands. I stifle a laugh. Jesus, what's it come to? I squeeze my way through the loved up clubbers and head for the toilets. The queue in the Ladies is massive and the average length of time spent in the cubicles is at least seven minutes. Probably crammed full of gaggling girls acquiring a new drug habit but no discretion. I mean no-one does it in the toilets in this place. No need. I head for the men's and have a piss. Some guy with dodgy shades on offers me Ketamine on the way out but I tell him where to put it. He calls me uptight but he's got that wrong.

I begin the squeeze again and eventually find myself in the chill out zone where Mr K and Jamie are entertaining Stace of all people with a handful of smarties.

''Ow much?' she asks. Mr K laughs deeply and puts one on her tongue, 'For you babe, they're free.'

Stace giggles and runs off to find her mate and I want to throw up. Instead I slip in next to Jamie and begin the transaction.

'How's it hanging Mavis?' Jamie asks, (that isn't my name, it's a greeting he uses for all females, God knows why).

'It's cool Jamie, it's hanging,' I say. (Well you have to talk the lingo with the natives don't you?)

'That's wicked Jay.' (Now that is my name, well sort of. At least it's what people call me and I don't object much and after all Jezebella is a bit of a mouthful).

'So what you been at Jamie?' I ask, trying to sound concerned.

'Oh you know, the usual,' he replies cutting some coke on the table with an old DSS Security Payment card. I wasn't really sure what the usual was at all but I said, 'Right,' as if I did.

I sniff a line through the rolled up twenty pound note Mr K hands me, swapping nostrils half way through. I eye the spliff he's been silently building and he hands it to me with a lighter and a smile, 'Spliff etiquette Jay?' he says.

'Cheers mate,' I say, giving him a cheeky grin, 'so how are you doin' Mr K?'

'Oh you know Jay, usual,' he replies in the standard answer. (OK so my mates aren't exactly riveting conversationally but they do have their benefits.)

'D'you reckon you could do me a couple of grams on tick until next week mate?' I ask Mr K, diving right in at the deep end and figuring if he's going to give pills away to strange fifteen year olds he won't begrudge me a few lines of sherbet.

'Hey, how can I refuse babe, when you ask me so sweetly!' he replies. I'm not sure if he is being sarcastic but he slides two wraps across the table anyway.

'Thanks mate,' I say quickly, 'I owe you one.'

'No,' Mr K says, 'you owe me a hundred and twenty.'

'Not a hundred?' I ask surprised at the rate of Mr K's inflation.

'It's good stuff,' he comes back. 'By Friday Jay, and I mean Friday.'

'Right,' I say, getting up.

'Where you going Jay?' Jamie asks sniffing, because he *has* just snorted shitloads of cocaine.

'I gotta fly mate, I've got a party to go to, later though.'

Jamie guesses what I'm on about and pulls me back, 'Don't do nothing stupid Jay, he aint worth it.'

'Trust me Jamie, would I do anything stupid?' I make my escape before the boys can argue, forcing my way through the club towards the exit and out into the night.

I zip my jacket up tightly and cross the empty road, trying to avoid the growing number of puddles. I look around for a second trying to remember where I parked the car and finally spot it lurking behind a camper van with daisies spattered across the paintwork and the words 'WOW YEAH' on the side. I tut at the stupidity and jump into the driver's seat, pumping the gas and roaring off past the prison. I slide a cassette into the stereo, 'Joyriders' by Pulp plays and I giggle to myself.

I love driving through London at this time. It's so easy. It's so fast. You only have to slow down when you spot the rozzers in a side street or you suspect a blue flash on your tail. You don't have to worry about speed cameras, that's all bollocks. I've had tons flash off at me and I never got a ticket for it yet. People say I drive like a man, whatever that's supposed to mean. I'm not quite sure how to take it. Does it mean I'm decisive or that I drive fast, or does it mean I'm a selfish, incompetent arsehole behind the wheel? I'm not sure. Anyway, I like the way I drive and it gets me places fast, like Wood Green for example where I am now.

I turn off the High Road and into Sylvan Avenue. Some wanker attempting and failing to reverse park, holds me up so I swerve round him. I park the car under a dark and shady tree and turn the engine and the lights off. I take off my red fleece and pull a black jumper stashed under the passenger seat over my head. I change my stacked blue trainers for a pair of flat black Reeboks hidden in the glove compartment. (That's what I like about Micras, big glove compartments). I put on the black woolly hat, not hidden anywhere, just left on the passenger seat, and tuck my short bleached hair inside it. I survey the street for dog walkers and slip out of the door, closing it gently to ensure no noise.

I open it again and jump back in having forgotten two important things. One: I pull one of the wraps from the right knee pocket of my combats and snort a bit from my thumbnail, licking up the spillage. Whoosh! Anaesthesia. Two: I put my hand under the driver seat and grab the bottle of paint stripper.

I step out of the car and close the door gently, survey the street for dog-walkers and begin my mission.

All is silent as I creep around the corner into the street I want. The lights are on at the house in question and I don't believe my luck. I was a little worried I wouldn't make it on time, knowing he's not one to stay up, even at parties. Perfect timing. I hide behind a tree and stare in. He's there, in the window, my ex-boyfriend Steven, champagne glass raised, lips puckered. I watch him clink his glass with *hers* and I watch them kiss. I can't see the ring but I'm sure it's sparkling beautifully. There are people all around them, cheering, clapping, a lot of people I don't know and a lot I do. People I once called friends. *'No way, Jay, we aren't going. Just fancy a quiet one tonight.'* Loyalty eh? I'm angry and I'm bitter but the coke numbs the pain I'm sure I'd feel otherwise.

I spy my target. Good. Perfect. Her red Mini is parked across the road by the park, right beside a tall bushy tree. This is ideal. I enter the park and stand behind the tree. I unscrew the top of the bottle and prepare. It only takes a second and the Nitromors is spilling from the roof down the Mini Advantage (well she took it). I consider scratching 'DIS' in front of the logo but chuckle at the idea instead. Good work, continue to phase two. I leave the park quickly but silently. The gate to the alley that runs along the back of the house is open and the fence is easy. I see my second target, ten yellow Dutch tulips, heads closed, swaying in the breeze. I jump down from the fence and I'm in. I pull the scissors from the side pocket of my combat trousers. You see, I only want the heads. It has to be precise and clean, otherwise they may blame an animal and Steven has to know it was me.

Snip, snip, snip, snip, snip, snip, snip, snip, snip, snip.

Done. Back over the fence, down the alley, through the open gate, down the street, round the corner into Sylvan Avenue, into the unlocked Micra and away into the night.

I deposit the car outside Curios, spotting a rather nice 50's dresser in the window, and walk the half mile back to bedsit land as quickly as I can, partly because it's getting very chilly and partly because the cocaine is making me rush and the adrenaline on top of that is an added bonus. Chewing my teeth in the cold night, I let myself in through the three totally un-secure front doors, put the first 'Baby Fox' CD on and lie down flat on the seventh hand mattress on the floor of my dusty room just off the Fortess Road. I picture Steven's face the next day when they see the car. Hell hath no fury? He didn't scorn me, he did me a favour.

I begin to feel a little silly about being so victorious over such a miniature protest. Messing up some slag's car and chopping the heads off a few tulips is hardly revenge, but it's got me feeling decidedly better. I had to give them something to mark their engagement.

Anyway, it wasn't my only revenge. When I went to pick up the rest of my things from the flat, after I'd moved out, she was staying over and they went out for a walk. He gave me an hour to *'Pack up and get out!'* I filled his bottle of salad dressing with crushed laxatives, pissed on her toothbrush and hid fish fingers under the floorboards in the bedroom hoping they'd go off when they turned the heat on. Oh and I shagged his best mate.

He shouldn't have messed me about. He knew I was the type with a taste for revenge but the thought of her brushing her teeth with my piss still got me going. Shouldn't have left her washbag lying about, stupid cow.

'She's a lot like you,' he said, the first time he plucked up the courage to admit to his infidelities. 'She likes Pulp a lot and she smokes Marlboro Lights.'

Wow, we could be sisters.

I wanted to throw out my Pulp CDs but hadn't the heart. Anyway I bet I'd been a fan a lot longer than her, having seen them in Sheffield eight years before. She probably only got into them after 'Common People.' I took up Marlboro reds the next day.

I heard her before I saw her. I heard her far too loud gasps as he shagged her in the bathroom a few days after he told me. He thought I was in Tring for the weekend. I sat in the kitchen and watched her face when she came out wearing his shirt (one I bought him for Christmas). She went bright red and I introduced myself. 'Hello,' I said kindly, 'you must Steven's latest bit of shag?' She just blushed and ran back to the bathroom. He started going to hers after that and I found a place to live.

'Bijou and compact,' I told my mate Genie, putting on a brave face, 'this is the living room *stroke* bedroom *stroke* kitchen and that's the shower in the cupboard.'

Genie inhaled the dank stench coming from the mouldy shower with zero ventilation and slid her slim hands through her black hair. 'Nice,' she said, giving away her distaste, 'very...'

'Small,' I offered. It was a bit of a come down after a two bed garden flat with stripped floors in the nice part of Wood Green. But it was home whether I liked it or not.

I don't miss Steven. I don't have time. I could have a different man in my bed every night of the week if I wanted and mostly I do. Nameless, faceless men. They rarely last more than a week and only get that far if they're lucky. I find them in bars looking for a good time and believe me they get it.

4. Bedsit Land

I sat on the bed with a soundtrack by Isaac Hayes and clicked the button on the answer phone, listening to the messages with as much attention as I could considering it was nine in the morning, I was on a come down and I'd had no sleep. I winced at the nasty computer voice telling me the time of the calls.

'Jay it's Genie—meet us for lunch if you fancy it, tomorrow, twoish yeah? Gis a call mate—bye.'

'It's me. (Who the fuck is me?) *What you up to babes? I haven't seen you since the Chelsea game. I miss you Jay. Why don't you return my calls? Please Jay? We gotta talk, I miss you. Call me yeah?'* (Oh, that me.)

'Jezebella it's your mother. Your father and I are sorting out some of your grandfather's business in London tomorrow so we'll pop by and see you first thing, about ten o'clock. Do make sure you're up early, you know your father can't stand it when you don't look presentable, oh and take out your nose ring darling, you know how he hates it. We'll see you at ten then alright?'

Shit! Ten o'clock. That gave me precisely fifty two minutes to tidy a room that looked like hell. I set about emptying roaches from the ashtray and hiding the mirror that was dusted in coke. I shoved my dirty clothes under the bed and tried to put the CDs back in the right boxes, giving up and settling on two piles, CDs and boxes. I ran round frantically trying to look at the crappy room with my father's critical Sicilian eyes and realised I couldn't do nish about the dirty duvet cover and the stained carpet. Most of the dirty washing up got shoved in the kitchen cupboard, but I had to wash three cups knowing they'd want tea. Great—no milk! Ran down the Seven Eleven, got milk, ran home, nine forty five, looked in the mirror.

I got changed fast, dirty crumpled clothes. I couldn't find a comb to run through my hair so I ruffled it up and hoped for the best. I completely forgot to wash the smudged mascara off my cheeks. I looked for my Lucio Battisti CD but couldn't find it so I put Umberto Tozzi on the stereo to put my Dad in a good mood, regretting it instantly as Umberto crooned his way through '*Ti'amo.*' Ding dong! Doorbell. Oh fuck!

'Hi Mum. Hi Dad.'

'Hello dear,' Mum said loud, then whispered sternly, 'I asked you to look decent.'

'You looka like you 'aven't shlept in a whola week.'

'Thanks Dad,' I said, spitting on my fingers and rubbing at the big black smudges under my eyes.

'She's upset about her grandad Totò, none of us have slept,' Mum snapped.

'Do you 'ave to wear thata ring through your nose like a pig?'

'Sorry Dad,' I said, realising that out of context I am very aware of my Dad's accent. I never noticed it much as a child but he really does sound like something out of a Spaghetti Western.

'Anyway, come in then, fancy a cup of tea?'

'No we can't stop Jezebella. We just wanted to see how you were,' Mum said.

Dad sat down on the kitchen chair. I tried to stop him because it could barely take my eight stone let alone my Dad's eighteen. There was a sickening crunch and a thud as Dad hit the floor.

'Sorry Dad, it's broken.'

Dad got up, rubbing his back and scowling at me like he did when I was a kid.

'Why do you nota bloody tell me isha broken? Are you trying to finisha me off?' He was well pissed off. He lit a cigar and turned his back on me.

'Totò don't smoke in here, the windows don't open,' Mum said.

'No that's fine Dad. I do,' I said.

'This is nice,' Mum said going across to the little cupboard in the corner I found in a skip.

'Yes,' I said, trying to get to it before my mother opened it and examined the contents.

Shit—too late.

'What's it like inside...oh...oh dear.'

'Jezebella, you don't, you don't *use* this?' my mother said holding up my nine inch, real feel, pink plastic vibrator in her shaking hand.

Mum didn't know where to put herself and I started laughing, more out of embarrassment than anything else. She pushed it back into the cupboard before Dad saw it and I have to say that was a relief.

'Come on Totò,' Mum said, her cheeks as red as my Dad's nose, 'we have to sort out Daddy's things.'

'We only justa bloody got 'ere,' Dad growled.

She grabbed him then and rushed out of the door, as if my depravity could contaminate her.

'Good bye,' she said curtly.

Dad just grunted, but he would.

Then I fell on the bed, wasted and cracked up.

I figured some weeks ago that the bedsit wasn't good for my self esteem and being alone so much wasn't good for my psychotic tendencies or my depression. Although the Paroxetene mostly kept my irrational desires at bay, there were still times when controlling my urges was hard work and I felt a change would be good for me. My doctor agreed and so I began to plan my escape. I felt that getting a job was be a good place to start, as £45 jobseeker's allowance each week doesn't get you much in the housing market. I couldn't do just anything though. It had to be quick fix and lots of money.

That was where Genie came in. She'd been working as the receptionist at a Kentish Town sauna for years. Fuelled by an array of store card debts and lured by the payrise, Genie had started doing some of the clients herself. She said if she couldn't tell me about it she'd go crazy and she knew I'd never judge her. Genie used to fill me in on the previous night's punters over black coffee and cigarettes in Banners, a favourite café of mine in Crouch End. (They did a nice line in bacon and mayonnaise sandwiches and good looking barmen, and you got as much black coffee as you could drink to go with it, great for a hangover.) Yeah, Banners was alright, as long as you felt able to deal with Psycho-Chef and the Crouch End witches. Psycho-Chef had chatted me up at the bar one night over cinnamon vodkas; he told me his name was Ivor and proceeded to describe every outfit I'd worn for a week and where I'd worn it. It was flattering at first but then when he told me where I lived it was slightly disturbing and I added it to my list of reasons to leave Crouch End.

Anyway, back to Genie. She was chain smoking her way through sixty B&H and eating mouthfuls of calimari in-between, when I said,

'So what are they like? I mean do you ever get any lookers?' She laughed then, spitting her calimari all over me and running her hands through her freshly dyed hair, (Raven No. 2 by Clairol), 'You must be joking love. Most of them look like a cross between Fred Flintstone, the Elephant Man and Woody Allen!'

'Nice,' I commented swallowing a mouthful of bitter black coffee.

'I mean,' she said, 'I wouldn't shag 'em if I didn't have debts.' Genie shovelled a forkful of calimari into her painted mouth.

I suppose I had this glamorised idea of doing it for money. Passionate sex in expensive hotel suites with Richard Gere, a couple of grand left on the bedside table. But Genie put me straight.

'So this geezer last night, he's about nineteen stone right. And his breath stinks of cigarettes. He takes me to this B&B in Finsbury Park. I'm sure he'd been wanking on the sheets for a week, it was gross. He wants me to go on top, which is all right 'cause I can shut my eyes, sit up and not have to be anywhere near his stinky face.'

Genie paused to swallow a hot mouthful of sweet coffee.

'Anyway, so I start and that, and he keeps pulling me down on him by my hair, trying to kiss me. I says, 'No way mister!' and he gets all narked, rolls on top of me, pins me down and starts pulling my hair and sticking his tongue down my throat. I fuckin' nearly puked all over the place!' Genie dragged hard on her cigarette and ground it to a halt in the ash tray, reaching for another. 'God he was vile, I aint doin' him again!'

I guessed then it wasn't the easy money I had figured and began to think about other ways to make a decent amount of dosh. I briefly considered waitressing but just as the thought crossed my mind Ivor emerged from the toilet, wearing his milk bottle glasses, ran his hand through his long greasy hair and threw me an enormous smile, his eyes roaming across my garb and resting in my cleavage. Fuck that, I thought. There's got to be safer ways to make money.

We left Banners amidst a torrent of whispers from the *witches*. (The Crouch End Witches were this group of young mothers who had nothing better to do than gossip about other people's lives, and I have to say that me and Genie seemed to be one of their favourite topics of conversation. According to those who'd been taken into their confidence, I had been in the local nut house for five years, was a smack addict and was responsible for the breakdown of every marriage in Crouch End. If a man strayed from his wife then either me or Genie had to be involved. It made us laugh big time. We used to fuel their gossip by talking complete rubbish at the table next to them and waiting to see how long the new version took to get back to us.) Anyway, I left them cackling their dull little lives away.

I was planning on going straight home to catch 'Sunset Beach' on Five, I mean there isn't much to do in Crouch End; but I quite fancied having a look round 'Squawk.' I'd noticed a retro 50's lamp in the window on my way to meet Genie and though I was certain I couldn't afford it I wanted a quick look. I had a thing about the 50's. My parents think I've got no ambition but I have: in an ideal world, if I had loads of money, here's what I'd do: run my own shop, packed full of 50's memorabilia, with a workshop at the back where I would renovate stuff.

When I lived in Tring with Jimmi and the others, while I was at art college in Wycombe studying furniture design, I found this 50's fridge dumped in the street outside some houses that were being done up. I got Bo to take it back to the squat for me in his van. The others laughed. It had been covered with wood-look sticky back plastic and white emulsion paint. Every night after college, I worked on that fridge, peeling and stripping until it gleamed bare metal at me. I resprayed it the original shade, a creamy yellow, and polished the metallic logo—PRESTCOLD, until it shone. She was beautiful, all curves and smooth lines. I changed the thermostat myself and tinkered with the motor until I heard that slow buzz. The other's didn't laugh then. We used it at the squat for six months, my 1952 Prestcold fridge/freezer, perfectly restored. All our mates admired it. They thought we were so funky living in a massive squat with an American style fridge. Then we all went to Glastonbury and one of Sasha's junkie mates said she'd house sit for us. We had to have someone there to keep the squat happening, and as everyone else we knew was either going with us or already there, she was the only option. She must have known it was worth something because she put an ad in Loot and sold my baby for three hundred quid. I actually cried. Sash said sorry. Where my fridge had once stood was the crumpled copy of Loot with the ad ringed in red. Three hundred quid? She was worth twice that.

Anyway, furniture restoration was my only skill but there was no way I wanted to work on boring old antiques for peanuts. I wanted to be my own boss or nothing, have a shop like Squawk. One day maybe. After all a girl can dream.

5. My Night With The Filth

Genie called me a couple of days later and said:

'Listen if you're still interested in making some dosh, I've got a proposition, meet me down the Maynard.'

And like a fool I did. I needed money, especially since I'd run up a debt with Mr K on top of my rent arrears and unpaid bills. Even though I didn't like the thought of getting mixed up in Genie's sordid tricks I wanted to hear her out. Well, at the very least I fancied a pint.

Genie found a seat and I ordered the round. The edited version of 'Creep' by Radiohead was blasting from the jukebox as I waited at the bar. Coming to the Maynard so soon after meeting Blondie was probably a mistake and when I saw him sitting on the same bar stool I knew it was.

'Chrissy?' he called to me. I'd forgotten the made up name and didn't register for a second.

'That's six pound twenty Jay,' Kiwi John said loudly, handing me my drinks. I gave him a tenner and mouthed 'Hi' to Blondie across the bar.

'Come over Chrissy,' he shouted back wanting to show me off to his mates who looked a right bunch.

I ignored his request, smiled and headed over to Genie. We started playing our usual game of Russian Roulette. I see a bloke

I fancy and I say to Genie,

'If he stands up and he's got combat trousers on, I'll shag him.'

We both tried to peer beneath his table, giggling like crazy. He stood up and was wearing jeans but I wasn't that bothered.

'Shame,' I said, 'he only looks about seventeen and I've always fancied getting myself a virgin!'

'No way mate!' Genie says, 'I'd rather sleep with someone who's had loads of people, then they know what they're doing. Mind you, right now I wouldn't mind giving up sex all together.' I wondered then if the prostitution stuff was getting her down but I didn't ask. Genie never talks about her feelings and she makes it pretty clear that she doesn't like people prying.

We started messing about with this keyring laser I chored off Jonni Lipshake, my hairdresser. I started shining it on the till screen every time this one barmaid went to ring up. (She's such a moody bitch! Genie started calling her Stroppy Knickers and the name stuck.) She started jumping back from the till, getting freaked out, trying to work out where the light was coming from. Then she turned round and saw me with it in my hand and shouted out over the din of the pub,

'Oi, you, stop shining that torch at me.'

Shame!

Me and Genie cracked up.

I chucked the laser back on the table and turned my attention to Genie.

'You won't have to do anything. He just wants another girl watching.'

'What, that's it?' I asked.

'Yeah,' Genie said, 'all you gotta do is watch me shaggin' 'im like.' She took a long swallow of her vodka martini and an uneasy silence sat between us for the first time ever.

'How much would I get?' I asked.

'Fifty,' she said, 'It'll only take ten minutes if that, he's not exactly one to 'old out! Jesus this drink is disgusting, I think they put sweet Martini in, should've gone to Florians.'

'I don't know Genie,' I said nervously, 'it's not really my thing.'

'Come on mate?' she pleaded, 'there's no-one else I can ask and if I don't sort it I'll lose a client.' Genie looked at me with begging eyes, 'Please Jay? I need the money. Anyway, he's a regular, I know him. I swear it'll be alright.'

I figured that the fifty would at least pay off part of my coke bill, and if I only had to watch... Anyway, I trusted Genie, she was my best mate.

'I'll think about it, alright,' I said and Genie smiled. We left the pub as fast as we could but Blondie was faster.

'Chrissy?' he said in a rather nauseating questioning tone, 'that number you gave me...'

'Look,' I said, 'I'm not interested alright.'

'You don't mean that,' Blondie said, 'we were so good together.'
Genie started giggling and I jabbed her in the ribs.

I had to laugh myself, Jesus what planet do men come from?

'I gave you head darling, don't get over excited.'

He looked a bit hurt and I felt bad for about point two of a
second, then Blondie pipes up, 'What's your problem Chrissy?'

'Urrr—nope, don't think I've got one!' I said.

'Why are you being so cold then?'

'Just leave it alright?' I said pushing past him and heading for
the door. I half expected him to shout something nasty but I'd
picked him well. I pushed my way outside dragging Genie with
me. After a couple more doubles at Florians Genie had convinced
me. She made a phone call and it was all set up. We took the
Triumph and drove back to her flat on Tottenham Lane an hour
before she was due to start work.

Genie lent me some of her work clothes. I actually thought I
looked pretty good in red patent leather thigh boots and a push
up bra, with eyes outlined in black and a blood red mouth. None
of it seemed real. My head was spinning from daytime drinking
and we were having a laugh trying the clothes on. By the time
we'd finished the half bottle of vodka Genie had in her freezer I

was totally up for it. Genie had two clients before she needed me so I hung around her flat, playing music and watching MTV until it was time.

I had twenty minutes to get to the Cross but the car wouldn't start and no amount of fiddling under the bonnet did any good. After ten minutes of trying I decided to find alternative transport for the night. I sorted that pretty easily and set off for the hotel wearing a big fur coat, borrowed from Genie's wardrobe, to cover my scanty outfit. A little nervous. I reapplied my lippy in the lav, had a quick line for courage then made my way up to the fifth floor, to room 509 where Genie was waiting with the punter.

He was a fat bald bloke with black rotten teeth and nasty tight briefs with a big elasticky waistband, the kind that'd look fab on some young male model with a great body but looked totally naff on him. He sat on the bed in his socks, Genie next to him in a red basque, suspenders and leopard skin print knickers. He had these nasty dark hairs on his shoulders and reminded me of an over excited ape. Thick globules of sweat ran down his neck and I could smell his stink from the door.

'Where the fuck have you been?' Genie said sounding very pissed off, 'you were meant to be here half an hour ago.'

'The car wouldn't start,' I said, standing in the doorway.

'Come on in then,' the punter said, 'and get your coat off

darling.' I let the coat drop to the floor and he let out a little gasp of excitement. I felt sick.

Then it started.

'I want to see you two kissing,' he said, licking his lips, spreading saliva across his chin.

I looked at Genie and she mouthed,

'I'll give you another ten.'

I walked across to her hesitantly. Her mouth tasted of cigarettes and chewing gum. My head started spinning again as the coke kicked in.

'Suck her tits,' he instructed Genie.

I was wishing I'd never got involved, but I didn't say anything. Genie let her mouth drop to my breasts and I stumbled backwards feeling faint. I think she thought I was pulling away and she whispered in my ear, 'It'll be over soon.' The man had his hands in his underwear and was playing with himself. But then he must have started to feel left out because he lunged at us pulling us apart.

'You,' he said pointing at me, 'you just watch right?'

I pulled away from Genie relieved, and leaned back against the wall at the foot of the bed. He pushed Genie down on the nylon bedspread and ripped at her knickers, tearing them on one side and leaving them hanging by her knees.

'Easy darlin',' she said her voice shaky, 'I thought you like me in control?'

'Not tonight,' he said, 'not tonight. Suck my cock—and no marks right, no marks.'

'Put the condom on then,' Genie said matter of factly.

'No,' the punter said, 'I want to feel your mouth.'

'Come on, you know I don't do that,' Genie protested, 'tell you what sexy, I'll put it on with my mouth shall I? You know you love it when I do that.'

'I want to feel your mouth,' he insisted. Genie looked scared and suddenly vulnerable.

He grabbed her hair and pushed her down on him.

'You watching this slag,' he called to me, 'come closer then.'

I didn't move an inch. Genie was gagging and choking.

'Look mate, she don't like that,' I intervened, 'stop hurting her.'

'Listen love I'm paying so shut it. Anyway, she loves it, don't you slag,' he shouted slapping Genie across the back of her head, 'Suck me harder you dirty little whore.'

Genie was still choking and her face was red. I moved across to the bed and attempted to get him away from her but he pushed me away and I fell, cracking my head against the cheap formica bedside cabinet. He was surprisingly strong for such a fat little man. As I got up I saw him turn Genie over and throw her bones down beneath him. 'I'm gonna fuck your arse slut,' he shouted pushing himself into her. He was going really crazy, losing it.

'Please,' Genie cried, 'not without a johnny. I'll do what you want, but not without a johnny.'

'You'll do what I want like it or not,' he said, pulling a knife from beneath the pillow and moving it towards Genie's throat.

'NO!' I shouted lunging at him, trying to pull him off Genie, who was screaming, tears streaming down her cheeks. My head was aching from the knock I'd taken and I stumbled towards them. I held onto his arm, digging my nails in, and Genie got free, she was crying hysterically and he had the knife at my throat.

'Come on then slag, come on then. Your turn is it?' he shouted, his saliva spattering my face.

'Come on cunt. I'm gonna fuck your arse now.'

I summoned all my strength and pushed him from me, the knife missing me by an inch and falling to the floor. Genie grabbed at it and held it towards him, her face red and angry.

'Get over by the wall,' she ordered, her ripped underwear and bedraggled appearance belying the calm of her voice.

'Fuck off!' he shouted at her.

'Get his wallet Jay,' Genie said, sniffing and wiping the tears from her face. 'We want paying Mister.'

'Let's just get out,' I shouted, wishing she hadn't used my name.

'Get the wallet,' she said again, her voice cold and hard.

'Leave it, let's just go,' I shouted again.

'Fucking get it Jay,' she said. Scared of the look in her eyes, I got the wallet out of his jacket and pushed it down my knickers.

'Fuck you, you whores,' he bellowed lunging towards Genie who held the knife outstretched.

I screamed and Genie screamed and the next thing I know the knife is in my hand and there's blood all over the bed and all over me and Genie and he's just lying there, not moving, claret all over the fuckin' shop, stuck to his nasty black hairs, shoving up through the sticky mess like spiders legs. I was standing there shaking and breathing hard and the room was spinning.

'Get the fuck out,' Genie shouted.

And we ran. Fast.

Down the dirty hall. Down the stairs. Coats covering blood-soaked underwear. Past the desk and the bored porter. Out the double doors. Out of breath and out of luck. Down the street, past St. Pancras, past the tube, past the garages hidden snugly beneath the arches of the railway bridge, past the taxis in for a service, past Keith's Hand Valet, into the car I came in parked on a yellow and then, and then...

'You stupid cow Jay! How could you come in a chored car tonight of all fuckin' nights?'

'I told you the Triumph wouldn't start and anyway I didn't know did I? Didn't know you were screwin' a psycho!' I held the wires together, my hands shaking uncontrollably, and sparked up the Fiat Brava.

'Just fuckin' drive then! DRIVE!'

Driving through the night and heading north as fast as we could, music blaring in my head, silence killing us, knowledge killing us, my heart thumping out some crazy rhythm, dump the car too close for comfort then run, left at the lights, down Kentish Town Road past Rio's the all night sauna—massage available, past the tube and the NK Convenience Store, past the Pizza place, ignore the wolf whistles from the delivery boys, quick step along the Fortess Road, through the door, into my block, up the creaking stairs, trip on the loose carpet, into my bedsit...bang, slam of the door, lock it, double lock it. Relief.

Shower in the mouldy cupboard, then panic. What do we do next? Burn our underwear? Wash away the blood? Hold each other through our distress? We fucked up big time.

I fucked up big time.

We sat in the dead silence of my bedsit.

'He was scum Genie,' I whispered, daring to talk first, 'he deserved it.'

'No Jay,' she said very slowly, her voice cracking and breaking, 'no-one deserves that.'

I didn't say anything then, just hugged the towel to my bruised body and stared at the floor. My hand was cut a bit and it was beginning to hurt though the bleeding had stopped. Genie stood up from the bed and crossed the room, looking out of the dusty window at the cars below, screaming through the darkness. She was wearing an old shirt of Jimmi's that I'd taken with me to London. Her thin legs were almost as white as the shirt and covered in goose bumps, bruises already forming and a patch of dry blood still clinging to her knee. She didn't turn to look at me, just spoke very quietly, her breath fogging the dirty glass,

'You lost it Jay. You went crazy in there. What is your problem?'

'I thought he was gonna kill you,' I said, pissed at her inability to understand, 'I thought we were both dead. He had the knife...'

'He wouldn't have used it Jay, he wouldn't,' she said.

'He did use it!' I shouted, 'he had it up against your neck and I...'

'Keep your fuckin' voice down alright?' she said.

'Alright,' I uttered through clenched and chattering teeth.

'What if he's not dead?' Genie spoke the words I didn't dare to, 'What then? It's me'll get banged up, not you, he doesn't know who the hell you are does he?'

'You won't get done,' I said, unscrewing the top of a bottle of vodka and taking a long swallow.

'Like you know that? What if I do?'

'What if, what if, what fuckin' if,' I said, well pissed off with her. 'What if I hadn't been there Genie and it was you lying dead in that scummy room?'

'He's got a wife and kids Jay. I'm his regular, there's probably people who know that. You were meant to watch, that's all, not knife him Jay.' Genie was getting a bit too hysterical for my liking.

'He's hardly gonna tell anyone he sees a tom is he?'

Genie remained silent and I passed her the vodka.

'Come on mate, you can't expect me to stand there and watch him do that to you. You can't.'

'It's my job isn't it? I'm a whore Jay, what do you think I do? This aint 'Pretty Woman'.'

In that moment I realised the gravity of the situation.

'Look Genie, just calm down alright. Please. It'll be OK. No-one'll give a fuck about scum like that. Another punter dead in a crappy hotel in the Cross. Who's gonna give a fuck? Not the filth that's for sure.'

'You don't get it do you?' Genie said, her voice cutting me, 'he *is* the filth. PC Phillip Murphy to be precise. You fucked up, you fucking fucked up,' Genie was pacing now, taking big gulps of vodka, and her face looked like hell.

'I should have known I couldn't trust you, I should have known,' Genie said, her eyes sparking. I shivered in the corner of the room, the damp towel chilling my icy flesh. I didn't feel a thing. I'd knifed some geezer, probably killed him and I didn't feel a thing.

'You fucked up,' Genie said again.

I could tell she was really scared. I moved across to the window and touched her back. She shrugged me away. I tried to put my arms around her but she pushed me away far too hard and I fell on to the messy bed.

'I thought he was going to kill you,' I said quietly.

'I know,' she said, 'I'm just so frightened.' I got up then and she turned and fell into my arms and I held her as tight as I could. We clung to each other for dear life and her tears fell warm upon my ice cold breasts. I took Genie across to the bed and we lay together with the duvet pulled up tight to our chins and our cold flesh gradually became warm again and sleep stole away the nightmare we'd been through. When I woke she was gone.

I didn't see Genie again. She decided it was for the best. She left me a note and seventy quid. I wished she hadn't left the money.

My head is spinning, my mouth is dry, sickness spreading through my limbs. I'm sweating and shaking, shivering, aching, breaking up again. There are wasps in my head, buzzing and whirring like radiohead when you wake up on acid, tuning in and turning on, spinning in my ears in the dark. My eyes focus slowly and the dark is full of colours. Full of red. Spiralling shapes of paranoid dreams. My skin sounds like sandpaper rubbing against these hollow sheets. Rescue me now, now when I need you. Now when I cannot stand to be alone.

I'm in Naples. I know that's where I am because the hot air is choking my breath. I can hear the chatter of cicadas through the open window and the muffled sounds of dust swirling beneath the feet of fast lizards. I am lying in a narrow bed and I try to place myself. I search the dark room for clues and find a mobile swinging by the open window. Paper aeroplanes dance in the still air. It's Fabrizio's room, my cousin Fabrizio's room and I am lying in his bed. I look down at myself slowly. I am wearing a pink nightie with tiny rabbits on it and I am ten years old.

I try to sit up in the narrow bed but the sheets have me trapped, tucked tight into their hot arms. I struggle hopelessly but I can't move. The door opens dreadfully and I am frozen. I watch some terrible dark figure move soundlessly towards the bed. 'Who is it?' I cry out, 'Clemmi? Clemmi is that you?' But the figure is taller than Clemmi and wider too. Suddenly I see the glint of metal in the figure's hand, shiny sharp metal aiming for my throat and in the light that is reflected I see his face.

I woke with a scream. I lay back in bed and shook. I lay in bed and prayed there would be no knocking at my door.

'No-one can prove we were there,' I told myself.

'No-one can prove that we weren't,' I said.

I decided in that instant that I have compulsive personality disorder—I compulsively screw up my life.

I thought about Italy. I needed money and fast.

I decided to write a list of all the things I was good at and see which one paid best.

6. Freaky Realistic

I had been walking for some time when I came upon a strange and empty place. I decided it was as good a place as any to sit and think about the mess I'd made and what my next move should be. My head was spinning, too full up. I went to buy cigarettes and swapped my returned to Marlboro Lights for the new and over advertised Marlboro Mediums.

'Just a short step from the Reds, girl,' Genie had said when I had hinted at the change a few weeks before.

'Yeah, but maybe I'll smoke less,' I offered.

'Yeah, *right*,' she said.

Anyway, I had made a definite decision and that was something, even if it only concerned the strength of cigarette I smoked. I bought the papers from the shop on the corner, found a car and went for a bit of a drive. I was trying to keep out of the bedsit as much as possible. I was shaky every time my doorbell went. I had no place to go, a lot of thinking to do and a whole lot of time to kill, so I drove around a few of the places I used to go when I was first in London and the world was a prettier place.

I drove up to Ally Pally and pulled over facing the edge of the railings where lovers park up at night, slipping a cassette into the stereo, 'Separations' by Pulp. I watched a man walking his dog into the distance and when he was no more than a speck I felt alone. I leaned back against the leather seat and watched London spin its dirty magic below. I watched the grey sea of the city with its foggy landmarks, rising high above Crouch End. Canary Wharf blinked hopelessly from the docks. Traffic streamed up and down the hills below. People going to work. Buses loaded with kids on their way to school. I watched it all from my metal cage, my breath fogging the glass, making soft edges of my sight.

The whole sordid scene with Genie had made everything a hell of a lot worse. I was most concerned by how little I felt about it. I had the images in my head: him naked and bleeding, his dirty underwear, his filthy smell, the sharp point of the knife piercing his skin, pushing through fat and flesh to find its home. But I kept on thinking he deserved it. I didn't feel bad and I didn't feel I'd done the wrong thing, though I knew Genie felt both.

I dumped the Jag and thought about Clemente for the first time in a week. About her state of mind and the hell-hole she lived in. About her crazy family and the dirty streets of down town Naples. Getting it together to get to Italy was a stupid idea in the first place and anyway, I'm shit at saving people, look at Jimmi and the others. Look at what happened with Genie. I tried to save her from death and she hated me for it. But if I could get to Italy, lay low for a while, then maybe, just maybe it would all go away.

I had to get back to the bedsit and sort out some clothes for the funeral, only a few hours away and in Birmingham of all places. Finding black clothes wasn't hard but finding clean ones was. I knew I looked a state but I wasn't too bothered. It wasn't about how I looked. It was about Grandpa.

By some miracle I got the Triumph started and drove over to Muswell Hill, following a faded map to my cousin Paul's place. I'd arranged to get a lift with him to the funeral because his car was more reliable than mine. I listened to *GLR* news and nearly crashed when I heard about the police constable found stabbed in a hotel room in King's Cross. Nearly hit a lamp post when they described him battling for his life in intensive care at UCH. *Police are looking for two women in their mid twenties. One is described as tall with dark, shoulder length hair and the other as small with bleached, cropped hair. Anyone with information should contact the incident room on...* I tried to push the fast approaching fear from my mind as I approached Paul's place. If I wasn't scared of what I'd done, I *was* scared of getting caught. I pulled over by a chemist and jumped out, leaving the car on a yellow. I bought two packs of Cherry Red hair dye and shoved them into my bag, jumping back into the car.

Paul lived in a housing association flat just off Cranley Gardens. I thought of Dennis Nielsen as I sped past his house of horror. All that killing going on within the walls of that tall grey building, tucked so neatly into middle class Muswell Hill. I'd read a book about him once and this one bit stood out: how he left a head on the stove simmering while he popped down the road to buy some Bacardi. No-one knew the truth of what he was because he just carried on as if it were any other day. All those men dead. Just another day.

When I got to the flat, Paul was sitting on a beanbag watching videos and eating a samosa out of a silver takeaway box. I'd never seen him eat before. He stood up when he saw me, all bones and teeth, like a dressed up skeleton.

'Hi Jay,' he said, 'make yourself at home.'

'We gotta go Paul, it's gonna take hours.'

'Yeah,' he said. 'Right.'

He pushed the rest of the samosa into his mouth, grease spilling down his pointed chin, and pulled on a black leather jacket.

'D'you think leather's OK?' he asked me.

'It's cool Paul let's go,' I said getting impatient.

'Yeah,' he said. 'Right.'

After he'd folded the sheets of toilet paper neatly enough and thrust them into his pocket, after he'd found the book on regression therapy he wanted to give to another cousin of ours and had shown me his skylight, we still hadn't found his car keys. I said I'd drive but he said his car was more reliable and carried on searching. I offered to hotwire the car but he didn't seem keen. An hour later we found his keys.

The M40 was a car park and his car was a mess. I sat in the passenger seat, hot sun baking my flesh through the windscreen. A half eaten sandwich curled on the dashboard, slowly fuming out the car with its pungent stench. Paul barely said a word the whole way, leaving me to suffocate in my murderous thoughts. By the time we got to Birmingham we were ten minutes late for the start of the service and we didn't have a clue where the crematorium was. Some woman with three kids in tow gave us the wrong directions and with Paul's strange manner of driving it took us another twenty minutes to find the place.

We ran across the grass and past the line of mourners awaiting their turn. Well, I ran; Paul did this strange skipping thing and I guessed he really had done too much acid in the seventies. I got through the chapel door in time to watch my Grandad's coffin sink out of sight to the sound of Pavarotti and to watch my family drift away through another door clutching their hankies.

'Fuck it, Paul,' I said, 'you should have let me hotwire it.'

Paul was so laid back he was practically horizontal.

'We're here man,' he said, 'he knows that, he knows. Anyway, at least we haven't missed the food. Come on let's squadge.'

I couldn't believe him. For fuck's sake man, we drive all the way to Birmingham in his clapped out Morris Minor for a few soggy sandwiches and a glass of sherry. I wanted the music and the church stuff, not to stand around talking to old dry people saying, 'Hasn't she changed? The last time I saw you you were, ooh, must have been, ooh, how old was she Derrick?'

I nibbled some crisps from the buffet which stuck in my throat like fish bones and said hello to all the people I should say hello to. Someone handed me a glass of wine and I noticed the shaking had started again. I wasn't cold but I was shivering uncontrollably.

'I thought you weren't coming Jezzy.'

I looked up into the dark eyes of my cousin Fabrizio and nearly spilt my drink.

'Fabrizio,' I said, trying to stop my voice from shaking. 'How are you?'

'Good, yes, fine. Work is going well. Think I might be a partner before the year is out.' His voice was matter of fact as if bragging was common practice to him.

'Great,' I said feigning enthusiasm.

'Mummy said you're living in London these days?'

'Yes,' I said, feeling uncomfortable beneath his gaze, 'it's been five years actually.'

'Whereabouts?'

'Tufnell Park,' I said defiantly, knowing he'd dis the area big style.

'Right,' he said. 'Not far from me then really?'

'No, not far.'

'So? Why haven't I had a visit?' Fabrizio asked fixing me with his Italian stallion looks.

'I mean, I always was your favourite cousin wasn't I Jezzy?' his hand lingered on the flesh of my arm as he spoke and I watched the goosebumps rise.

'How's Clemmi?' I asked changing the subject.

'Not good. Mummy's going through hell with her. She's totally flipped. She won't even speak to me. Anyway, enough about my little sister, want a lift back to London in my new car?'

'No, thanks Fabi, no,' I answered quickly.

'It's a Porsche!' he said looking very pleased with himself. 'You always did love fast cars!'

'I've got a lift thanks.'

Fabi laughed loudly, 'What in Paul's relic? Come on Jezzy? Don't you fancy doing a hundred and fifty down the M6 with me? I'll even let you drive a bit if you're good.'

'I have to speak to Mum Fabi, sorry, I'll catch you later yeah?'

I disappeared into the adjacent room to find Mum. Fabi was making me uncomfortable. Mum was looking pale and tired in her grieving garb. I wasn't too used to seeing my mother get emotional. She was always so cold, so in control. But she really looked like she was going through it and I have to say I felt concerned. I scanned the room but Dad was nowhere to be seen. I wondered if he'd managed to find an excuse Mum would accept.

Mum was chatting to a work colleague, one of the nurses from her ward I think, a fat woman with red cheeks and too much blue eye shadow. I overheard a few sentimental sentences about Grandpa before interrupting. Mum looked at me outraged by my rudeness, barging in to their private recollections. And I suspect she was still reeling from the shock of discovering that her only daughter masturbates with a battery operated device!

I couldn't face the return journey with Paul and I wanted to get back to London and sort things so I borrowed a tenner for the train off my mother, apologised profusely, blamed Paul and got the fuck out. I found an empty carriage on the train, lit a cigarette and examined the list of things I am good at.

Things I'm Good At
1. Growing Hemp plants.
2. Giving blow-jobs.
3. Choring cars.
4. Breaking into houses.
5. Tequila drinking competitions.
6. Sleeping.

7.   Predicting the future.
8.   Cooking Hot-pot, poached eggs and Duck à l'Orange.
9.   Chatting up men.
10.   Masturbation.
11.   Wallowing in the past.
12.   Getting into trouble.
13.   Obtaining expensive goods without expense.

Well, I thought, coming up with thirteen things I was good at was pretty cool. Only problem was that four of them were highly illegal, three involved sex and I'd already been down that route with Genie, five you couldn't make a living out of and as for becoming a chef... Well my repertoire didn't even stretch to McDonald's and to be honest my Duck à l'Orange is more like Chicken Drumsticks with Marmalade, a favourite recipe of my mother's, and let's face it she aint the greatest cook on this planet; the only person I know who can burn a poached egg.

I screwed up the bit of paper and threw it out of the train window. I wasn't too keen on doing something illegal as a profession but it didn't seem I had much choice. It's not a moral thing I can assure you, I just figured I was in enough trouble as it was without totally taking the piss out of the rozzers.

When I got back to the bedsit I dyed my hair red, spattering dye over the mouldy tiles. I watched my reflection in the mouldy mirror, feeling like some cliché criminal in a bad film. Like a change of hair colour would stop them finding me. I gripped the cold rim of the sink with shaking hands and looked into my own eyes. I looked as hard as I could though I am not sure what I was looking for. Nothing had changed about me. I was paler maybe, a bit thinner than usual. There were tired shadows and dark circles but that was normal.

When I was a kid I used to stare into the mirror for ages, trying to scare myself. I was looking for something then too though I never found it. It was like when you stare at flames and see pictures. I was waiting for my face to change, for some demon to manifest itself right before my eyes. Catholic guilt I suppose. I pushed my hair back with my hands and sighed. I felt as if I was beyond help. I couldn't turn to anyone because I couldn't tell the truth. Genie was my last link with sanity and she'd made her feelings clear. I had a sudden urge to call Jimmi. Not to tell him or anything, just to chat. I wanted his mindless chatter to make things real again.

I picked up the phone and began to dial, realising it was a very long time since we'd spoken. I watched my fingers punching in the numbers. I let the phone drop back down. On the back of my left hand was a small red stain, slipping in between my thumb and forefinger onto my palm. I turned my hand over slowly and it began to shake. My palm was a mess of red hair dye that had leaked through the thin plastic gloves. A deep red stain in the palm of my hand and it may as well have been blood. I found the bottle of bleach tucked behind the toilet and fought with its childproof lid, tipping the thick liquid onto my hands and rubbing until the stain disappeared. I stood with my hands beneath the hot tap until it was too hot to bear.

Then I began to make plans. I had this contact. His name was Howard but he called himself Felty. Well, his associates called him Felty because he'd spent most of his short life in Feltham Young Offenders Institution. Anyway, Felty had this thing going, this scam. He had a mate with a garage. Him and his mates chored cars, good ones, and his mate changed the odd chassis number, the plates, bit of a re-spray. The result was a car worthy of flogging and making a fair amount of wonga. Felt knew how good I was at choring cars—he taught me everything I knew, back in the getting to London and changing my life days. Back in the Crouch End flat share days. We'd had a summer of fun, joyriding London in fast convertibles, making easy money. Then Felt got nicked and went down for a two stretch. Visiting him in Brixton kind of wore the glamour off and I stopped doing it for money. Too many connections getting made, too many people getting scared and opening their mouths for a deal. But Felty knew I had what it took and besides, no-one ever suspected girls. He'd tried to get me in on it a few times since but I'd told him quite firmly that I didn't do it for dosh. I did it for kicks and to go places I couldn't get to without a set of wheels, like when the Triumph was fucked or something.

Anyway, I figured this was different. I had no morals about it, nothing like that, I just couldn't be bothered getting into a ring and the subsequent knock, knock, knocking at my front door. Felt said I'd get a grand for every decent car I chored. If I could do a couple, I figured that'd be enough dosh for a return flight to Naples and some cash to keep me sweet while I was in Italy.

I packed my gear that night. I didn't take much, I didn't want the rozzers thinking I'd scarpered if they searched the bedsit. I sat on the bed with my passport in my hands and wondered what I'd do when I got there. I thought about Clemmi and whether she'd come away with me. I knew I had to go. I had no choice.

By the following evening I was ready. Flight booked, Felt and Danny D. waiting with the cash and a plan of action worthy of Ronnie Biggs. I knew where to get good cars. I knew the hotel car parks and the posh bars. I knew the double yellows outside the Atlantic or the Groucho Club. I knew the dirty bastards that could afford to own and insure that kind of automobile and I knew they didn't deserve it.

I chose a Z3 roadster 3.2, arctic silver with round spoke alloys, electric soft top and personal plates that read; SEX 1. Bit risky but worth it to see Felt's face. I drove towards Finsbury Park and got to the garage at ten. Felt laughed his arse off. Danny D. just said, 'Stupid cow! Didn't he tell you? No personal plates right?'

Me and Felt were laughing too hard to care. 'You gotta admit it mate, she's good,' Felt said, putting his arm around me. Felt wanted to shag me in the Z3 just for a laugh, said he'd never done it with a *ging-er* but Danny D. was already pulling the seats out and I had to chore at least another one. In the mess of death around me, sex was the last thing on my mind.

'Wanna come Felty?' I asked. 'I fancy a Rolls tonight!'

'All right Jay,' he said, 'but only if we can do a bit of sinning on the back seat, that new hair colour of yours is turning me on!'

'No way man, no way,' Danny D. butted in, like we was serious, 'no fuckin' Rolls all right? Get me a Chimaera, a 4.0, I've got a scrapped one out the back.'

'Boring!' I said.

'D'you want the dosh or not?' he asked.

I walked out then and Felt followed me.

'Fancy a beer?' Felt called out.

'No ta,' I said, looking back and winking, 'I don't drink and drive!' Felt almost pissed himself laughing then.

We stopped at the Maynard and found Irrelevant Pinchcock sitting on a split leather chair by the pool table. Doyen of the Maynard posse and slave to its whims, Pinch observed the push and pull frenzy of football fans through his pint of bitter shandy and said to no-one in particular, 'I saw it coming. The football renaissance, didn't I tell you so?'

Felt went to get the beers in and I approached Pinch.

'All right geezer?' I said, mimicking his South London drawl.

'No. No I aint all right Jay,' Pinch said looking very pissed off indeed. 'My flat is full of smackies and I says to them, 'Get that scag off my fucking breadboard,' but they don't. I had to get out. It's getting ridiculous Jay. I mean a smoke now and then yeah, no problem, don't do it myself, but no objection. But they're caning it mate, started injecting and everything. I can't live like that man, I can't do it.'

Pinch has one of those faces you really like but you don't know quite why. I never forget the first time I met him; after about twenty minutes I said, 'So what's your real name then Pinch?'

He answered in his usual flat tone, 'It's irrelevant.'

'No seriously,' I said, 'what is it?'

'It is,' he answered slowly as if I was a bit stupid, 'irrelevant.' And that's how he got his name I guess.

Pinch swallowed the remainder of his beer and went to the bar. I shouted after him, 'Hey, Pinch? Felty'll get ya one. Felty, get the man a pint, he's got the smackies at his place.'

Irrelevant Pinchcock turned to me then and said very clearly, 'Ya don't HAVE to tell the whole pub Jay, it aint necessary.'

'Sorry mate,' I said, surveying the crowd around the pool table.

Felicity Feelgood preened her blonde bush with red nailed glory and slipped her index finger across the head of her half pint of Guinness. She sucked the creamy foam from her finger and half a dozen men nearly came on the spot. She looked up at the screen with wide blue eyes and said,

'He's got nice legs that Ryan Giggs.'

Intellectual Plughole sighed deeply, raised his head from his textbook on Euro-Centrism and said,

'Oh puleeze!' in his totally phony but unfortunately real deep south American accent. 'It's a game of football not a talent quest!'

Felicity Feelgood giggled loudly and looking for an ally, leaned towards me and whispered, 'Lots of talent though, eh Jay, especially that Giggsy.'

'He's alright,' I said, 'good footballer and that; Beckham's better though, but he's alright.'

'Alright?' said Felicity, 'Alright? I tell you, I wouldn't kick 'im out of bed if he farted!' Poor Felicity, she probably owned one of those baby sized football shirts which she squeezed her tits into to get the lads going.

Felt came back with the beers and three packets of 'Salt and Linekar' crisps. Pinch grabbed a packet and walked up to the bar. He shouted across to the bored bar maid (Stroppy Knickers) in a loud voice, 'I didn't ask for *Salt and Linekar*, I asked for *Salt and VINEGAR*. She shrugged, picking at her nail varnish and said, 'Same fing'.

'It aint,' said Pinch, 'it aint the same thing at all. If I wanted dodgy footballer flavour crisps I'd ask for them, all right?' He threw them back at her and returned to our table by the pinball machine. Felt was going into one about some car he chored from Stokey that Danny wouldn't take. I said, 'I better get cash Felty, I got a plane to catch.'

'Well he aint gonna give you a cheque is he?' Felt said.

I shut up then, feeling a bit stupid and Pinch started on about the frigging crisps again.

'I mean you don't get *Smokey Beckham* do ya? I hate Gary Linekar. I aint eating no crisps flavoured wiv him.'

'You been hanging out with the Smack Boys too long,' Felty said. 'Anyway you get *Cheese and Owen* now doncha? They'll be doin' *Smoky Beckham* before you know it.'

'What about *Worcester-Shearer Sauce*?' I said chipping in.

'*Teddy Salted*!' Felty said laughing loudly.

'I don't get that,' Felicity said looking confused.

'Teddy Sheringham,' I said but her face was blank. 'Here Felty what about *Roast Le Boeuf*?'

'Nice one Jay! Nice one!' Felty said laughing again. Pinch didn't look too happy about our Walker's advertising campaign brain storming session.

'BASTARD JUNKIES,' he shouted and stormed out.

Me and Felty ignored him and picked up our drinks. I put it down to his excessive E intake, we were all coming down with that. Fuck knows what Felt put it down to, he didn't say a word, just slurped his pint of cider.

'How can you drink that shit?' I asked.

He rolled a joint and ignored me. I swallowed the warm remains of my bottle of Becks. I felt like everything had changed. I couldn't relax. I was trying to have a laugh with my mates, act like everything was alright but the futility of their conversations grated. Arguments about crisps and football players. Getting pissed up and pissed off. I didn't want any of it. I wanted a plane ticket to Italy. I stood up. 'Come on mate, we got work to do,' I said walking towards the door. When I turned back to look for Felt he was chatting up Felicity Feelgood in her tight pink mini skirt and fluffy angora top with sequin motif. I didn't argue.

It must have been my fucking birthday because I got myself a red Chimaera not far from the boozer and drove it over to Danny D. I panicked when I saw the rozzers on my tail. You hear about people getting caught like that. Wanted for murder and caught doing something far less significant. The police turned off after a mile or so of my 'safe' driving and I guessed I was being paranoid. I passed Prospero's Books and All Bar One, crawling along at 30 with the other dickheads. Then I sped out of Crouch End and over to the garage, down Stroud Green Road at ninety five and then some, past the queue of people outside La Porchetta.

Danny and his mates had turned the Z3 over by the time I got there and it was ready for the paint shop.

'Good work Jay,' Danny said, looking genuinely pleased and handing me an envelope stuffed with cash. I counted it carefully because I didn't trust him one inch. It was fifty short and I pulled him up on it. He feigned surprise and blamed a mate, pulling a fifty out of his jean pocket. I scarpered. I had a plane to catch. He shouted after me, 'If you fancy it as a regular thing Jay?' I didn't answer. I don't plan to end up with a lead role in Car Wars.

7. Bella Italia

When I stepped off the plane I realised I had made a fatal error. I had forgotten to bring my address book and so I had no means of contacting Clemmi. My only options were either to just turn up at the house or to call my mother, and to be totally honest I wasn't too keen on her knowing I was in Italy. Eventually I settled on the telephone directory and I discovered that by some freak of nature Italians were not quite so paranoid about stalkers or freaky phone calls as Brits, and Zia Joanna was listed. The phone rang and rang but there was no answer.

I hailed a taxi and found myself close to death in the back of a Fiat Uno heading for the rough end of Naples. By the time I reached Via Pazzo I felt decidedly sick and not much like saving anyone. But Clemmi was my cousin and I'd been like a big sister to her back when we were kids and she still lived in England. I paid the crazy cabby and headed for number 13, unlucky for some and probably for me.

When I reached the door my head flooded with a thousand childhood memories: all the times I had arrived at their front door, brimful of excitement at seeing Clemmi, brimful of dread at seeing Joanna or Claudio drunk out of their minds and ready for grief. I pulled at the knocker cautiously. Joanna answered, clutching a tumbler of Vino Rosa. She didn't have a clue who I was and started gesticulating and telling me to '*Vaffanculo.*'

'*Zia,*' I said, '*Sono Io, Jezebella.*'

Joanna squinted at me, reverted to English, 'Jezzybelly? My God!'

'*Zia,*' I said, embarrassing her cautiously.

'Jezzy? You should have told us you were coming.'

I noticed that all the years she'd been living in Italy had done little to erase her English accent.

'*CLEMENTE,*' she screamed, '*VIEN QUI ADESSO!*'

I was still standing on the doorstep when Clemmi came down.

She stood behind Joanna and stared at me with blank eyes. She didn't say a word and I wondered if she'd forgotten how to speak English. I wondered if she had forgotten who I was. I wanted to say, 'Clemmi, it's me, it's me Jezzy,' but I couldn't speak any more than she could. Joanna hustled me in then shouting to my uncle, 'Claudio! Claudio! We have visitor from Ingleterra.'

As I entered the living room I noticed Zio Claudio passed out on the sofa, huge pasta-filled belly lolling out of his vest, bottle of beer still in hand, empty grappa bottle balanced on the edge of the table. Jesus, he looked like my Dad. He snorted loudly and spilt the dregs of his beer on the floor. Joanna disappeared into the kitchen singing 'Sunny Goodge Street' by Donovan.

'Clemmi?' I said, looking at the brittle bony figure that I

vaguely recognised.

'Clemmi? It's me, Jezzy.'

'Lo so,' she said. I wanted to shake her, I wanted more than "I know," I wanted joy and happiness. I wanted her to feel her saviour had come, but all I got was blank eyed nothing.

Joanna came back with a fresh bottle of wine and a broken cup.

'Sorry Jezzybelly,' she said, 'no clean ones.'

'That's all right,' I answered squirming at the sound of my childhood name. Claudio let out a loud grunt and Joanna whispered in her slurry voice, 'Let's try the kitch-kitchen girls. Don't want to wake Papa do we?'

I followed Joanna into the kitchen which I hadn't seen for at least ten years. It was a total dive. Worse than the squat ever was. I didn't like to say anything but I was beginning to think I'd made a big mistake. I wasn't surprised Clemmi was mid breakdown. It wouldn't be hard to lose the plot living with them.

'So Jezzy,' Joanna said slurring my name terribly, 'how's my darling sister?'

'Oh, you know, bearing up,' I said imagining Mum's pale face the last time I saw her.

'Was the funeral lovely darling?' Joanna's English accent was as theatrical as ever, 'I was so upset about Daddy's death but I couldn't afford the flight, not with Claudio out of work and all that.' Joanna topped up my wine which I hadn't even sipped, rubbed a tear from her eye and got to the point.

'Has the will been read yet?'

'I don't know Aunty, I don't really have much to do with family stuff these days.'

'Well tell your mother to phone me the second it's all sorted out.'

'I will, yes,' I said quickly.

I turned to look at my cousin who was sitting with her head in her hands and her hair all over her face.

'How've you been Clemmi?' I asked as lightly as I could.

Before she could open her mouth Joanna said,

'She's a fucking mess, *è proprio una vergogna*, don't talk to her.'

Clemmi shouted at her mother, '*Testa di cazzo*,' and ran out of the room. I heard the front door slam and sighed loudly.

'What's going on Aunty?' I asked.

Joanna began to mop invisible tears from her eyes, her head lolling forwards, 'She's gone mad, Jezzy, she walks the streets at all hours, doesn't know what day it is. She started seeing some crazy therapist who's been putting ideas in her head. Making her think things happened that never happened.'

'Like what?' I asked, bemused and intrigued.

Joanna ignored my question, 'She's given up everything. Her job, everything.'

Joanna started crying for real then and I wasn't sure I could handle an alcoholic aunt right then.

'I'll go after her Zia,' I said getting up.'

'NO—leave her. She's crazy, *fuori di testa, pazza, matta, instabile*!'

To be honest I didn't fancy walking the streets of Naples looking for Clemente anyway. I fancied a couple of tokes and a warm bed and maybe a plane out of Naples. I'd rather be on the run in London than hang out in this godforsaken city. But I went anyway. As I left, Joanna was shouting, 'I've had enough, *basta, basta smettila.*'

I ignored her and ran out into the street towards the piazza.

I was pretty shaken seeing Clem like that. Bright, pretty, sparky Clemente. That's how people talked about her. I wasn't sure who this drab, worn out person was, masquerading as my cousin. I wanted to know where all the life had gone, all the sparkle. I thought about all the times when we were kids when Clemmi was there for me. All the sweet little things she did.

When I was eleven Clemmi came over to England for Christmas. She stayed at Granny and Grandpa's which wasn't too far from Tring so we saw each other every day of the holidays. Sometimes I stayed there too, and Clemmi and I would whisper in the dark about boys and music. Granny had decided we should

have a party so Clemmi could meet all my friends. We planned it
for weeks. Granny hired the village hall and Mum booked Dave
Dazzler's mobile disco. I invited all my school friends.

Mum bought Clemmi and me new outfits from the
underground market in Aylesbury. I had this frilly white blouse,
new romantic style with matching knickerbockers in burgundy
and gold. Clemmi got a kilt in the same material and a burgundy
top. We looked brilliant. I wore my pixie boots and sparkly silver
tights. We dyed our hair with burgundy wash in wash out hair
dye. Clemmi's didn't show because her hair was jet black, but
mine, being a light brown in those days, went bright red. Dad
went mad and made me wash it twelve times but it still didn't
come out.

When the day came, we were so excited. I'd invited Adrian
Burne who was the best looking boy at school. He had flicked
hair with a rats tail and loved Duran Duran as much as I did. I
just knew his best friend Gavin would be mad about Clemmi.
Adrian had been my boyfriend for two whole weeks. He'd bought
me a blue metallic plastic chain which I wore with pride. I danced
with Clemmi in full view of the door, waiting anxiously for
Adrian and Gavin. I got Dave Dazzler to play 'Girls on Film' and
Adrian arrived right on cue.

Gavin took one look at Clemmi and asked her to dance right

away. I grabbed Adrian and smiled at him stupidly while we moved to the music. When the song was finished Adrian went off and I chatted to some friends. I tried to find him but he was nowhere to be seen. Clemmi came and helped and we went to look in the kitchenette bit at the back. Adrian was there alright, his mouth clamped to Lindsay Riley's, his hand down her top. I stormed out to the toilet crying and Clemmi followed me. On the way Gavin stopped her and asked her to dance. 'No thank you,' she said, following me. I knew she really fancied him and her rejection of him showed me how much she cared about me.

We stood in front of the chipped mirror and I stared at my red-faced reflection. Clemmi tried to mop the sticky slicks of blue mascara from my cheeks and handed me her lip gloss. 'Come on,' she said, 'we don't need stupid boys to have a good time.' Just then the record changed and we heard Barbara Gaskin singing 'It's my party', and we both burst out laughing. We spent the rest of the night 'ignoring' the boys and dancing our socks off.

That was Clemmi. That was the strong, selfless girl I had known.

I found Clemmi in the square as I'd guessed I would, sitting on the church steps where we used to sit swapping secrets in the hot sun. She looked like a child sitting there, her thin arms wrapped tight around her slim frame, her long black hair falling over her tear filled eyes. I sat down next to her without saying a word. I put my arm around her shoulders and wiped the tears from her cheeks with my sleeve.

I didn't know what to say so I started singing an Italian song she used to like when we were kids.

'*Gi sondra cocodrile e due orango tango, due picoli serpente, un aquilla reale, gatto, toppo, elephante...*'

Clemmi smiled and sniffed.

'*E, ti va di mangiare?*' I said in a strong *Napoletano* accent. Clemmi laughed a tiny laugh, pushing her hair from her face. I took her hand and pulled her up.

'Come on. I fancy *uno gelato al melone senza panna.*' I spoke in the very English accent as I'd had as a child, to make her laugh.

'Jezzy?' she said, 'oh Jezzy!' She collapsed in my arms like a child, crying her heart out and soaking my shoulder. I held her tight and she shook. We stayed that way until the shaking stopped and her tears dried up. I pulled away and looked at her face. I wiped away the last of the tears with the cuff of my jacket and pulled the joint I'd been rolling on my way to the Piazza from behind my ear, put it in her mouth and said, 'Fancy uno spliffo?!'

Clemmi laughed and smudged her mascara across her fragile cheek bones with the back of her hand.

'*Canna,*' she said, '*canna.*'

'I wondered what it was in Italian, not the kind of thing Papa taught me!' I said, sparking up my lighter.

We walked to the *gelateria* smoking the joint, me singing the childhood song in a funny Neapolitan accent, the English channel and the Swiss Alps keeping me safe from my own troubles. I bought Clemmi a melon ice-cream and forced her to eat it while trying to ease her problems out of her. As far as I could see she wasn't the least bit crazy, just stressed out and depressed and in need of a change.

She asked about the funeral and laughed weakly at my late arrival. 'Typical!' she said. She reckoned Paul's mum, Great Aunty Pamela, was getting revenge from beyond the grave. Pamela was always late for everything and it used to annoy Grandpa like crazy.

'Fabi was there,' I said.

Clemmi didn't answer.

'Why have you two fallen out then? Is it one of those stupid Italian family feuds?'

Again Clemmi was silent. I decided it might be a good idea to change the subject so I ranted on about how much Naples had changed since I was last there and asked if Clemmi had been over to Sicily to see the family in Palermo.

Clemmi gradually became more chatty and by the time we reached Pazzo Street Joanna and Claudio were dead to the world and Clemmi and I were getting on like we always did. We sat in her room where we had slept as children and I told her my plan.

'I want you to come away with me Clem?' I said cautiously.

'Why?' she asked quietly, her features soft in the muted lamplight.

'Because Naples isn't good for you right now, and this house is the last place you need to be.'

'I can't,' she said, 'Mummy needs me.'

'What your mum needs is to dry out. Come on Clem, she doesn't give a toss about you.'

Clemente looked sad then and I got a bit worried in case I'd gone too far.

'Look, we'll go to Sicily for a while, OK? A couple of months, we'll drive around. We can live it up in Palermo, it'll be fun. You can sort your head out.'

'Then what?' she said, her eyes full of pain.

'I don't know,' I said.

'I want to get away from here,' she said quickly, 'but not Sicily. It isn't far enough.'

'Well, Milan then or Firenze,' I offered.

'No Jezzy, not Italy. Take me back to England with you.'

I said nothing for a moment. I had come here for Clemmi, of course I had, but there were other reasons too. I couldn't go back.

'Clem, it's tricky. I left England because I had to,' I said.

'Why?' she asked, her voice concerned.

'I just needed to get away for a while,' I answered quietly.

'But you have to go back sometime,' she said. 'We can go tonight. If I stay in Italy Papa will find me. He'll make me come back here. I want to go far away Jezzy, far away.'

I watched all my plans falling down about me. 'Somewhere else then,' I suggested, 'what about France or Switzerland?'

Clemmi shook her head, 'Please Jezzy, I want to go back to England. I was born there, it's my home. There's something I need to do there. I just want to go home.'

I watched the sadness in her eyes. I watched the pictures in my mind. Forensic photos of knife wounds. My mother crying in a courtroom. Genie's eyes full of hate and fear. Me lying on a narrow grey bunk in HMP Holloway waiting for the scream of the siren so I can walk the deadbeat circle of the exercise yard for half an hour.

Clemmi's voice full of suffering broke into my thoughts, 'Do you remember when we were kids and you said you'd do anything for me, no matter what? Do this for me now Jezzy? Please, do this for me now.'

'Alright,' I said reluctantly, 'we'll go tonight.'

Clemmi hugged me, 'Thank you Jezzy, for coming to get me.'

I held her tight and wondered what the hell I was going to do. I decided that Clemmi and I would lay low at the bedsit for a day at most and then get on a train to Manchester. I knew people up there. If I was out of London I'd be OK. Well, that was what I kept telling myself.

'Hey you'll be able to see Fabi again,' I said, 'and my Mum and Dad.'

Clemmi didn't answer and I hoped mentioning Fabi again wasn't a bad move. When I mentioned his name, her eyes sparked up, cat like. I began to pack her things and eventually she joined me. When the bags were zipped up I helped her write a note to Joanna and we sneaked out of the front door and headed for the airport. I thought about all the times I'd been through that airport, arriving happy, leaving in tears.

I was about nine, maybe ten. Mum and Dad had brought me to Italy even though I didn't want to go because it meant I would miss a whole summer of fun with my friends. All the way to the airport I'd sulked. Seeing Clemmi would be good but the thought of staying in the same house as Fabrizio and Joanna and Claudio filled me with dread. Mum and Dad had a hotel room but I had to stay there. Clemmi was upset with her mum over something or other and we decided to run away. We packed our bags, took some cold pizza and pretended to go to bed, but we jumped out

of the window and ran off into the crazy streets of Naples. We
didn't get very far before a *caribiniere* picked us up and took us
home. Dad and Claudio were furious. Claudio took it upon
himself to beat us both for it so when Dad came over I got a
second bashing. I remember Fabi laughing at us when he opened
the door, saying, 'Dad's gonna kill you—you two are *morte*!'

There wasn't a plane we could catch for three hours so we
attempted to get some sleep on the nasty plastic chairs in the
departure lounge. I still had over a grand left in cash so I fell
asleep planning how to make it last.

Just as I was drifting off I heard our flight being called on the
tannoy. Clemmi had vanished.

'*Volo numero 2342 diretto a Londra*,' the metallic voice
repeated.

'CLEMENTE!' I called out, scanning the greasy lounge. Jesus
Christ, maybe the girl is crazy after all. I went over to the enquiry
desk and got a call put out. Then I checked the toilets, just in case.

Clemmi had her head in the sink and was throwing up some vile
black liquid and the melon ice-cream. 'Hurry up, they've called
our flight,' I said grabbing her shoulders. As she rinsed her mouth
under the cold water tap, I caught my reflection, surprised by the
newly dyed red hair in the mirror. Clemmi plunged her hand into
her pocket and pulled out a bottle of pills, swallowed five and

looked up at me. Her eyes were puffy and her face was a mess. 'I'm ready now,' she said quite simply.

'Well, come on then,' I said dragging her and our bags along towards the departure gate. The tannoy blurted in its tinny voice, *'La Signorina Rossi Clemente è desiderata al banco Alitalia situato nella zona A.'*

'Thanks anyway, I found her,' I shouted at the receptionist behind her neat plastic desk, forgetting to speak in Italian.

'Che?' she shouted back, obviously confused.

We got on the plane and I held Clemmi's hand until she fell asleep. I tried hard not to think about the troubles waiting for me back in England. I began to think that maybe I should have persuaded Clem to go to Sicily. Stayed in Italy, just as far away from Naples as we could get. But I knew that I owed her. I had made a promise when I was ten and I couldn't break it now. I comforted myself with the fact that I had more than enough money for a train to Manchester.

I watched the cloud formations and wondered about the weather in England. I very much doubted the sun was shining the way it did in Italy. My prediction was as accurate as ever and as we circled Heathrow, I watched the grey clouds turn black.

8. London Calling

When the plane touched down in London I swallowed the melted remains of my double vodka and tonic and took off my seatbelt. The two flights had begun to take their toll and I was exhausted. I decided not to wake Clemmi until we were ready to disembark. She wouldn't be able to handle all that hanging around stuff.

When the air hostess announced it was time to get off the plane I called to Clemmi and prodded her lightly. She came round slowly and asked where we were in Italian. I told her we were in England and she looked a bit shocked, as if the past ten hours were a dream.

The tubes were fucked, (person under train), so we got a cab outside the airport and the driver was fairly quiet which pleased me no end. We slept in the cab and woke up outside the Pizza Hut which was only a few doors from my gaff. I wasn't sure how Clemmi would greet Bedsit Land but I guessed she'd prefer it to the hellhole she'd been living in with Claudio and Joanna.

I was pretty scared about entering the flat. I had images in my head of some police officer sitting there, waiting for me. 'Jezzebella Rossi, I am arresting you for the attempted murder of some filthy scum, you do not have to say anything but anything you do say will be used to crucify you.'

I opened the door slowly and breathed a sigh of relief when I saw that nothing had changed. We were both pretty wasted but I skinned up anyway, more out of habit than need. We smoked the joint and fell asleep on the mattress, waking at five in the morning to retrieve the covers and warm our shivering limbs. I got up twice to check the lock on the door.

I woke again at ten and crept from the bed to make coffee and left Clemmi sleeping. I closed the sliding partition between the room and the kitchenette and retrieved the packet of Lavazza from the fridge. When the coffee was bubbling up through the *mocha* I sat shivering on the small stool, the only one I had, and took small sharp sips of the thick black liquid, burning my tongue with the first and cautiously slurping the steaming caffeine afterwards. Clemmi was making sounds in her sleep. Frightening sounds, like disaster was imminent. She woke with a scream and I leapt to her rescue and roused her from her tortured dreams.

'*Dove sono?*' Clemmi said.

'You're with me, Clem, in London.' I answered stroking her hair, 'You want coffee?'

'*Si,*' she answered, '*grazie tanto.*'

'*Prego,*' I answered, going for the coffee. '*Zucchero?*' I asked, thinking she'd be in need of the extra energy.

'*Quattro,*' she said.

'*Quattro?*' I asked.

'*Quattro*,' she answered.

I took the coffee to her bedside and put some music on. My hand quivered by Nick Cave which suited my mood, but settled on No Man, chilled but far more upbeat. I thought Nick Cave might just send Clemmi over the edge.

I decided to try and talk to Clem about her troubles, hoping it wasn't too soon. I sat down beside her on the bed and took her hand in mine.

'I've missed you Clemmi,' I said. 'When I heard, I mean Mum said that you...' I didn't know how to say it. Mum had told me that Clemmi had lost it, gone 'cuckoo' as she put it. I wasn't sure if people who were mentally ill knew that they were. I mean I see a doctor for depression and that, but it's hardly the same thing. Mum had made it clear that Clemmi had flipped out, totally lost it. I tried again, 'Mum said you haven't been yourself lately. I want to help Clemmi.'

I didn't think I'd done too badly and when she started to talk I was certain I was the right person to help her.

'I can't seem to feel happy anymore,' she said slowly, trying to find the words in English.

'Did something happen?' I asked, 'something that started all this?' Clemmi looked up at me and her eyes filled with tears. I squeezed her hand and prompted her.

'Clemmi, you can tell me anything, anything at all. I won't tell anyone, it's between you and me alright, secret, like when we were kids.'

Clemmi spoke painfully, cautiously, her voice thick with tears, 'I cry all the time. I can't help it or stop it. I just keep crying and it hurts me. I see *dottore*, how you say Jezzy?'

'Doctor,' I said.

'A special doctor. She helps me to remember things.'

'Like a psychiatrist?' I asked.

'Yes, I think, like that, psy…chiatrist. I see her for four months now and it makes me very… *tristej, depressa*. She makes me understand things that have happened, in the… *passato?*'

'Past,' I said.

'Yes past, sorry Jezzy, I am very tired and my English is not very good now, but I want to speak in English to you. We always talked in English when we were… before.'

'It's alright Clemmi,' I said reassuring her, 'take your time OK?'

She began to speak again, with her eyes closed as if it might make her invisible, as if she could not bear to be seen while speaking of these terrible things.

'It is something that happened a long time ago, when I was very small and now that I *riccordo*, remember this thing, I can't be happy.' The tears began to tumble down her cheeks and I scanned the room for some tissues settling on a roll of recycled toilet paper. I tore off a long strip of sheets and handed them to Clemmi. She began to dab at her wet cheeks. As she let her hands fall on to her lap I noticed her left wrist was a mass of criss cross scars, some deeper than others, raised above her pale skin. I wondered what had driven her to mutilate herself so horribly.

'What is it you remember Clemmi?' I asked gently.

Just as Clemmi opened her mouth to speak there was a loud knock at the door.

'Who the fuck?' I said getting up, hoping it was Mark from upstairs or someone else I could get rid of fast. I opened the door reluctantly.

'Jay?' Jimmi said, opening his arms out to me.

'Jimmi?'

I couldn't believe it, I mean he always had lousy timing but not now man, not now.

'I'm sorry Jay, I had to come.'

Jimmi pushed past me into the room, dropping a fat rucksack by the door. There were tears in his eyes and he looked awful. He didn't seem to notice Clemmi but I could see her peeking out from beneath the covers and then rapidly pulling them over her head. He was pacing the room, smoking furiously and looking a bit peculiar.

'Jimmi,' I said, 'it's not a good time.'

'Hey, babe, I aint got nowhere else to go.'

'Oh fuck,' I said, 'fucking hell Jimmi. I've got company.'

He turned to view the shape beneath the crumpled bedclothes.

'Oh great Jay, great, didn't take you long. Thought we had somefing going Jay. Somefing good Jay?' He was virtually hysterical, still pacing, pacing and shaking.

'Jimmi? I've been here five years! I've lived with two men since I left you! Was I s'posed to wait for you to get your shit going? Anyway it's my cousin, Jimmi, my cousin.'

'Always knew you was a bit pervy,' Jimmi said looking sulky and pulling out a packet of Rizlas and twenty Marlboro, cigarette smoked right down to the filter still in his hand.

'Get the fuck out Jimmi, this aint the time,' I said feeling angry at his pathetic sulkiness.

'Look Jay, I didn't mean to fuck you off man. I'm sorry, just let me stay a couple of nights yeah, till I can get sorted.'

Well what could I do? I mean mates are mates and he wasn't to know about Clemmi and let's face it, if she weren't here I'd be pretty thrilled to have Jimmi here, so I could show him how much I'd changed and how much I didn't need those wankers back home. And maybe, just maybe 'cause I still cared for him. Anyway, he could stay permanently if he wanted to. I was going to Manchester with Clem.

I ushered Jimmi out of the door and made him wait in the hall while I explained to Clemmi what was going on. She seemed relieved to not have to talk anymore. I promised I'd be back and Jimmi and I went to Fat Sam's café to grab a cup of tea and a greasy bacon sarni or two. As the air hit my face I almost felt relieved to get away from Clemmi's tortured presence, instantly feeling guilty for the thought.

'How are the others?' I asked hesitantly, as we found a table.

'Not good Jay,' he answered looking into his tea cup for answers.

'Why?' I asked, 'what's up?'

'It's Sasha,' Jimmi's eyes filled up with tears again. I wasn't sure I could take much more crying. 'She died Jay. I wanted to tell you myself. Didn't want you to hear it on the vine, you know.'

'Fuck,' I said, though I wasn't shocked. Sash had a thing about death. She always said it would come early for her and the way she lived her life made that pretty likely. I didn't need to ask what she died of, well maybe the specific drug, but I could pretty much guess that too.

'Bad smack,' Jimmi said, wiping his eyes, 'she went off to Wycombe one night with some geezers we didn't know, blokes she met in the Black Horse. Some security man found her at the back of the Octogon, just lying there man. They must have dumped her after.' Jimmi covered his face with his hands, crying hard. I imagined Sasha's body, lying in a pile of rubbish, cold and dead. An old woman in the corner was staring at us.

'When, I mean, how long ago Jimmi?'

'Last week, uh... Tuesday night,' he said, running his hand through his grown out bleached hair, tears spilling into his tea.

'Why didn't you call me straight away?' I asked feeling hurt.

'I did,' Jimmi said, 'there was no answer and you know I hate machines.'

I left it then recalling where I'd been on Tuesday night. I felt suddenly weighed down. Death was circling, getting closer all the time. It'll be me next I thought. It'll be me.

'How's Bo taking it?' I questioned knowing the answer wouldn't be good.

'Dunno. He legged it man, straight after the rozzers came round. Haven't seen him since.'

'Fuck!' I said. 'Fuck.'

'Johnny went back to his mum's, couldn't handle it without Sash there.'

'When's the funeral?' I asked.

'Today,' Jimmi said, 'two o'clock. I couldn't face it, that's why I came here, I can't do it Jay. You have to let me stay with you.

You're the only one who understands me Jay, I need you.' I took both his hands in mine and held them tightly, looking into his watery green eyes, almost falling in again.

'Jimmi,' I said firmly, 'she was our mate, we have to go.'

I felt bad. I hadn't seen Sasha in over a year and I knew I'd failed her. Jimmi looked like shit. I knew what he was like. He probably hadn't slept since Tuesday. He'd probably sat there on his own in his room smoking himself stupid, drinking Red Stripe. 'We'll go this morning, back to Tring. We'll get the others and we'll go to the funeral.'

'OK,' he said, 'but I'm comin' back with you after, if that's all right. I can't stay there man, not without Sash.'

'We'll see,' I said. 'How's Ziggy taking it?'

'Not as bad as when Skag went. Bad, I guess. You know Ziggy, don't say much.'

'No,' I said.

Our sandwiches arrived and Jimmi ate mine as well as his own because I couldn't stomach it. Death was all around me and I didn't like it much.

'Look, I'm going back to the flat. Give me twenty minutes with Clem before you come back, then we'll sort it all out OK?'

'Sure,' Jimmi said, bacon grease dripping from his lips. 'See ya then Jay.'

I plodded back to the bedsit, stopping at the shop on the corner to buy food. When I got in I didn't see Clemmi at first, then I noticed her crouched in the corner shivering. I tried to explain the situation as best I could, filled the fridge up, grabbed some black clothes still lying around from Grandpa's funeral and said, 'I'll be back tonight, just stay here Clemmi, OK? There's food in the fridge. Just don't leave all right?'

'All right,' she said, almost sounding pleased, 'really, I'll be fine.' I was a bit worried about the sanity of her answer but right then I didn't have much choice, I mean I had to go to Sasha's send-off and there was no way I could take Clem, the last thing she needed was a funeral.

Jimmi turned up half an hour later looking a bit stoned and I went out to fiddle with the car in the hope I could get it to Tring and back. I got it started which was a good sign and it seemed alright. As Jimmi and I climbed into the Triumph I considered locking Clemmi in but the cruelty of such an action scared the shit out of me. In the end I settled on running back up the stairs to reassure her before setting off for the bleak hills of Hertfordshire and that nasty little town that used to be home.

9. A Funeral, An Engagement and A One Night Stand

Second funeral in as many weeks, the rain poured down my neck as I stood and watched the wooden casket judder into the ground. Sasha's mum was clinging to the green carpet at the graveside, meant to disguise the dirty earth and its cold hard cruelty. It just reminded me of grocery shops. She wept as loud as a person could and Sasha's sister, who was something in advertising in Milton Keynes, attempted to haul her to her feet.

The Catholic priest had tried to say as much good as he could about Sasha and settled on the idea she had been led astray by evil drug pushers. Her sister scowled at me and Zig, Jimmi and Johnny, right through the service as if it had all been our fault. The church was pretty empty and Bo didn't show up. We opened and closed our mouths to the hymns and sat and stood as told. There was little feeling and I knew it wasn't the way Sash would have wanted it. She had written her own funeral, as if she'd known, starting with The Clash singing 'Should I Stay Or Should I Go' and ending with 'Lay Me Low' by Nick Cave. Her mother wouldn't hear of it; Catholic Mass, 'Jerusalem' and 'Abide With Me' being far more suitable for her junkie daughter.

We'd all decided to give Sasha the send-off she would have wanted when the others were gone and this charade was over.

'Peace be with you,' the priest said.

'And also with you,' Sasha's relatives replied crossing themselves. I suppressed the inbred urge to cross myself because God hadn't been around me in a long time.

The mourners disappeared towards their cars and the prospect of sherry and sandwiches. Jimmi, Johnny, me and Zig stayed behind as the gravediggers began to fill the dirty hole. Sasha's mum passed us and yelled, 'It's all your fault you drug addicts!'

Jimmi gave the gravediggers a tenner, borrowed off me, to take a break, rolled a spliff and passed it round before beginning the service we'd planned for Sash in the car on the way back to Tring. Johnny pulled the crappy tape player from our old room out from his coat, like Fagin, and the funeral began.

'Dearly beloved,' Jimmi started, reading from Sasha's hand-written funeral service, 'we are gathered here today to say goodbye to a dear friend, Sasha Jane 'Spliff head' O'Heaney. Sasha's time on this earth was cut short by some bad shit, but we will all recall what a bright, if stoned, individual she was, a friend to her dealers and lover to Bo.' Sasha's humorous words jarred with Jimmi's tear stained voice.

'Let us stand for the first piece of music, selected by Sasha prior to her death, made bearable only by the high she would have felt shortly before. Let us be stood for 'Should I stay or should I go'.'

The tinny sound, almost swallowed by the wind, bleated out from the cheap stereo. We all sang along and pogo'd round the grave, Johnny playing the odd bit of air guitar, tears streaming down our faces, images of Sasha buzzing through.

'And now,' Jimmi said, 'I would like to read a poem written by Sash, some months before her death;

No future, no money,
The dole isn't funny,
Listen to music,
Go to a rave,
Buy a few tabs
From gorgeous Dave,
Go down the boozer,
Get looked at like a loser,
Drink a few beers,
                    I want out of here.
Give Bo head
and go to bed.
Get up at twelve
Smoke a joint
Tell me friends
What is the point?
Life? It's crap.

'Sad words, I am sure you will all agree.'

We all bowed our heads, and I was pretty sure I was not the only one who was trying to smother a giggle at Sasha's appalling literary skills.

'And now, let us dance once more and sing along to Sasha's favourite song of all time, 'Chinese Takeaway' by Ipswich band, The Addicts.'

"Hey Hey I want a Chinese Takeaway,
Hey Hey, a wo, wo, wo,
I went to the fish shop
Bop bop de bop
I went to the chip shop,
Bop bop de bop,
I went to the burger shop,
Didn't have a long stop,
Bop bop de bop..."

The gravediggers, eating sandwiches by the churchyard wall, were looking at us as if we were total idiots, dancing round a half filled grave, smoking joints and singing along to 80's punk songs but it was what Sash wanted and I guessed she was having a far better time than she'd had in the preceding hour and a half.

Jimmi said a few more not so carefully selected words and we all stood silently for Nick Cave's 'Lay Me Low', our heads bowed. Ziggy took out a bag and we all delved in to select an item we thought Sash might want in the afterlife.

'I'll miss you mate,' Zig whispered throwing a packet of Jelly Babies into the grave, 'I'll always remember how much you liked these. Bye Sash, until we are reunited.'

'Nice one Zig,' Johnny said, patting him on the back.

Sash and I were running fast along Brighton Beach. It was two in the morning and we were just coming up. Ziggy, Johnny, Bo and Jimmi were splashing about at the edge of the sea. We fell down on the shingle giggling like children and Sash pulled the bag of Jelly Babies from the knee pocket of her combats. We devoured the whole packet in minutes, chewing the sugary sweets and picking bits out of our teeth.

'I love Jelly Babies!' Sash said.

'I know Sash,' I said, 'You always say that when we're tripping.'

'Do I?' she asked.

'Yes and then you always say "Do I?" when I tell you that.'

'How can you remember a thing like that when you're tripping?' Sash said.

'I dunno, just do, and you always ask that too!' I answered.

Then we fell about laughing again.

The boys were singing really loud and Jimmi was jumping waves. I laughed at his persistence.

'You really love him don't you?' Sash said out of nowhere.

'Too right mate,' I said, lightening up the conversation, concerned by her serious tone.

'Why?' she said then and I thought about it.

'Because... because he's gorgeous, funny, exciting... sun-shiny, lip smacking, thirst quenching... Jimmi is it!'

Sash looked at me then, dead serious, despite my humorous jingle to Jimmi,

'Don't let him get away Jay. You aint gonna find that again.'

'I won't Sash,' I said, knowing I would leave him before the year was out. We went quiet then.

We were watching the West Pier and we hadn't spoken for ages. Then Sasha's voice came out of the thick silence broken intermittently by the distant sound of the waves and the laughter of the boys, doing their 'bonding on acid' trip.

'It's like a ghost building, isn't it?'

'Yeah,' I answered knowing exactly what she meant.

'Wouldn't it be great to watch it burn,' she said, 'see all that beauty just sinking into the sea in a blaze of flames.'

'Don't tell Bo,' I joked, 'you know he'd do anything for you.'

'Wouldn't that be great Jay! If someone loved you that much, loved you so fucking much they'd set the West Pier alight just so you could watch it on acid!'

I listened to her talking and was overwhelmed by the urge to do it. To run to the nearest petrol station and fill up the can from the back of the car. To swim out there and tip the sweet smelling liquid all over that wreckage, to put the flame of my Zippo to it and watch it burn and fall away. To make Sasha's wish come true. I thought about it as long and hard as you do when you're tripping and then, distracted by the boys charging us, let the thought go.

Jimmi and the others jumped us then, tipping coca cola into our open mouths and down our necks. Sticky brown liquid seeping into our T-shirts. Jimmi kissed me and his lips were sticky too. I lost myself in the feel of his mouth. Sash was right, me and Jimmi pulled some pretty wicked shapes together. We lay there on our backs watching the stars breathe and the moon spin her silver shadows. We listened to the waves crash and as the tide I turned to him then.

'I love you Jimmi,' I said.

'Ditto,' he answered giggling at my seriousness.

'I mean it Jimmi,' I said sitting up, 'I fucking mean it.'

Jimmi touched my face with his hand and let it fall across my shoulder and down my back, outlining the curve of my spine. I felt the tingle of his touch rush through me and I fell into him.

When I looked up again Sash and Bo were gone and Ziggy was completely mashed, flat on his back examining the shape of his hand against the moon. Johnny was sitting further down the beach staring at a shell he'd found an hour before. The next thing I knew the West Pier was crumbling away into the sea, a huge blazing inferno illuminating the dark sky and Sash was spinning round and round on the shingle shouting, '*I love you Bo!*'

Johnny went next, throwing a book in, 'This is for you Sash, for your poetry and that. I'll miss your spliffs man, really miss them, sleep good girl.' The pages of the book fluttered in the wind and I read the title. It was Sylvia Plath's 'Ariel' collection. The front cover showed a vase of bright red tulips, tall and proud with one lone flower hanging sadly, head bowed to the ground.

I had chosen Sasha's collection of pipes, nicked way back on a trip to Camden market. 'I want one from every stall!' she'd said lining her pockets.

'See ya Sash, keep smokin' girl,' I said, 'I'll miss you.'

Jimmi had selected Sasha's blue rubber dress, on Bo's behalf really. It was her favourite item of clothing which her mother had refused point blank to bury her in, 'here you are mate, slip it on you sex kitten!' Jimmi said, just the way he used to.

We were all at F.L.Y. and Sash was at the bar getting water. I watched her slink through the crowd, tight in rubber, tripping on her stacked trainers.

'Here you go mate,' she said, handing me the bottle, 'you coming up yet?'

'Certainly am,' I said, unscrewing the top and swallowing long and hard.

'Where are the others?' Sash said looking into the crowd.

'Dancing,' I said. 'Dr. Hugo's started playing downstairs.'

'What are we waiting for?' Sasha pulled me from my seat.

We began the trek towards the basement level Subvert room, passing assorted friends and strangers on the way. When we reached our destination a heaving mass of bodies moved to the sounds spinning on the decks. Sash dragged me towards the front, up by the DJ booth and we started to dance. We were both on pink callies courtesy of Uncle Bob and the rush was good. Sash was going for it big time, dancing her tits off. I watched her face as I danced, watched her lose herself in it. I watched the shine of the UV on her rubber clad body. She was really something. Only Sash could get away with a dress like that at a party like this.

She grinned at me and I grinned back, stupid E smiles. The boys spotted us and came over. The music was kicking and we were all having it. 'Biggin' it large style,' Sasha said and I laughed.

Sash put her arms round me and shouted in my ear above the track, 'I fuckin' love you Jay!'

I laughed at her pill talking.

'I mean it mate, I mean I know I'm loved up and that but I do, I fuckin' love you.'

'Me you too Sash,' I shouted still laughing. Dr. Hugo was mixing like a God and we slipped into the sounds of Scope.

'I fuckin' love this track,' Sash said pulling me further into the depths of the crowd as 'Tongue in Chic' played.

'I fuckin' love this party!' she said. 'Thanks for bringing us Jay, you're the best.'

'Me you too Sash,' I said to the coffin below. We left the grave with our arms around each other, sharing a soaking hanky on the walk to the King's Arms. Well, we hadn't been invited to the official wake and it wasn't really our scene anyway so we settled on smoky bacon crisps and warm lager in the local.

We slouched around the table like a gang of Goths in our black garb, only Jimmi's brand new and far too red *Adidas* trainers blighting the image.

'To Sash,' Johnny said morosely, raising his pint.

'Sash,' we all mumbled, swallowing our drinks.

The pub was a bad place to be that afternoon; there was some engagement party going on in the back and they'd got the monopoly on the jukebox for the day, which meant we had to endure the Spice Girls and Boyzone for two hours and cries of, 'To Debbie and Davy, aahhhh!' and drunken staggerings and letchings as assorted men undid their flies and fiddled with their tackle on their way to the gents, unfortunately placed behind our table. Then there was a fight between one of the party and a local lad with a skinhead haircut and a pint of Guinness. In the end we headed back to the squat feeling worse.

Johnny and Zig had decided to find Bo, who they considered would be feeling suicidal, so they set out on their mission leaving Jimmi and me alone. Nothing much had changed. The owner had legitimised the arrangement a while back with a rental agreement, but everyone still called it 'the squat'.

'Just like the old days eh?' Jimmi said, unsurely.

'Not quite,' I replied quietly.

'No,' Jimmi said, 'I guess not.'

'I better get going,' I said quickly, searching the room for my bag, 'it's a hell of a trip in the rain with that car, roof leaks and everything.'

'Not yet,' Jimmi said, crossing the room towards me, 'stay tonight?'

'I can't Jimmi, it's not right, and anyway there's Clemmi.'

'Well stay for a bit then.'

'A bit of what Jimmi?' I said sarcastically.

He looked hurt and I regretted my flippancy almost immediately. The truth was he still had a huge effect on me despite my catalogue of failed relationships and one night stands in London. I made for the door but Jimmi stopped me and trapped me against it, pushing his bones against mine. He bit my lips with his teeth and I felt the salt sting taste of blood on my tongue. I tried to protest but the thought of his naked form, spread across the bed in candlelight, all tight and warm made me lose control. I needed human contact. I needed to warm my ice cold flesh. We rolled into the bedroom we used to share, a half dressed tangled mess of desire. I inhaled the musty smell of his unwashed skin and tasted his sweet sweat in my mouth.

'Tell me I'm still best,' he whispered in my ear in that sexy fucking bastard way he had. 'Tell me I'm the best.'

'You're the best,' I said feeling the excitement of the moment surging through my veins like smack, 'the best Jimmi,' I whispered, out of breath.

'Tell me how you like it girl, come on, tell me how you like it or I'll stop.'

'Don't stop Jimmi please?'

'Then tell me,' he said grabbing my hair and pushing me down, 'tell me how you like it?'

'Hard Jimmi, I like it hard,' I said remembering the lines.

'And...' Jimmi said.

'And fast, fast, hard and... fast.'

'Good girl,' Jimmi whispered, 'keep saying it, keep saying it baby.'

'Hard and...fast...and...hard...and...and...fast...and...hard... and...oh Jimmi, harder...faster...faster!'

We came together in some huge explosive relief of years and grief and the proximity of death. Jimmi clung to my body like a child until I rolled away and I felt the same sicky feeling I used to feel in the old days when I wished he'd said, 'I love you' when he was coming instead of, 'Fuck me you bitch, fuck me!

Fleeting time is lost in the rain of tears spent on you. The years of waste. I am no longer crying. I made a life for myself; it may not be much but it's something. I watch the ceiling, a faded blue blanket of colour, caught in the half light. I shield my sighs with soft warm hands. Am I removed now, from your muddled mind? Or do I twist and turn it still as you do mine? Slowly learning death again. I am bare. Sculpted by you amongst others. Soft, porcelain clay made flesh by rough hands. You mould me until I can no longer speak. My tongue is as torn as my flesh. Torn by long fingered hands. Sharp and warm, it stings. Not even the rain can burn me so. I am scared. That is the truth. I am scared of death and of what I have done.

I live by soft light with you gone. Your life is little but fragments. You are too fast in the first place. You could walk the streets all day in the rain and I could drive fast cars but our thoughts would probably be the same. All I want is some peace of mind. Why can't anyone tell me which piece is mine?

'I have to go,' I said, lighting the half smoked joint that lay discarded in the ashtray.

'Not yet Jay?'

'Come on Jimmi, don't give me shit, I've got to get back to town,' I said dressing quickly and using my knickers to clean myself.

'I'm coming with you Jay,' he said half heartedly.

'No Jimmi,' I said quietly, 'you're not,' but wishing he was.

He didn't say another word and I wasn't listening anyway. I grabbed my jacket and left, heading for the King's Arms where I'd left the car. The rain was falling gently on my face, little flying splinters that speared what was left of my heart.

It won't leave. It spins and turns through the rain,
this dis-ease. This disease.

When will the rotting stop and the beauty begin again? Little blue pills. Little sweets that keep me sweet most days. Take them away and I'm crawling the walls. Take them away and I couldn't live without you. Don't let me taste this because I know I'll want more. Don't let me down because I know I couldn't take it again.

I will drive back to London and you will stay there in Tring, that hole we used to call home. In the silence of that dead place that sits too close to the heart of the triangle. Trapped in that pretty tree ring. It's too magical for you anyway.

10. Found and Lost

By the time I hit the M1 the rain was torrential and my windscreen wipers were doing overtime, going so fast I thought they might fly off into the night. I could hardly see a thing but I kept up the pace anxious to get back to the flat and to find Clemmi safe and sound. Pissed off by the lurch in my stomach every time an image of Jimmi naked on those dirty sheets spun into my head. I tried to push the thoughts away and concentrate on Clemmi and what the hell I was going to do with her. But those hours in his bed had given me a taste again. The come down from leaving him was already fucking with my head. I needed another fix already and the withdrawal was worse, worse than the side effects of taking Jimmi ever were. I'd kicked that habit once already and I didn't like the thought I was hooked all over again after one crappy fix.

It fucked me off big time that I couldn't stop thinking about him. About his beautiful fragility. About the deep sea swell of his green eyes. About the darkness of his hair beneath the bleached spiky ends and the shape of his lips which invited me towards him so unequivocally. About the way that when he's there I cannot look at or think about any other. I recalled the way that he bit my tattoo, with such precision. The way he bit into my lips and kissed me so fucking hard and fast like nothing else I had ever felt

in my life, and it made me sick. I stood in that pub and any one
of ten men would have given anything to spend the night with me
but all I had eyes for was him. All I wanted was him. His mad
crazy ways and his unthoughtful fuck me harder faster harder
faster thing. And I wanted so much to walk away and not care,
not give a toss but I couldn't could I? Could I?

No I couldn't. Because.

Because Jimmi was everything. The way he was with me. The
way he held me. The way he looked at me. The way he would fix
me with those eyes, those eyes and I would be completely lost. I
would drown, there and then in his gaze. He only had to look that
look and I would be lost. Lost to the wave of desire and guilt.
Lost to that swell and swerve of longing, of rich and full on want
and need. Lost in his secret pleasure trove. He burnt me. Burnt me
with his brutality and the fullness of his cravings. He could stand
a mile away from me and I would still feel the burn.

We used to speak on the phone when we were apart and he
could do it all and more with his voice. He could send me reeling
over the edge with his dirty talk. He knew every button he should
push and he did. I'd say, 'How you doing?' and he'd say, 'Wanting
you to suck me baby, suck me hard and fast,' and there I would
be. Lost. Again. Lost in the longing, the push and pull of it. The
empty feeling that swept through me when he wasn't there. When

I needed him there. I'd known Jimmi longer than anyone, since we were kids. There had always been this thing between us, this inexplicable bond. We used to joke that we were brother and sister, we were that close. When he was in pain I used to feel it too, feel it cut through me. I would have taken his pain if I could. I thought about all the times we'd been close. All the times we'd been there for each other.

Jimmi was laughing loud and I was running.

I was being pursued by a swarm of nasty black flies attracted to the shiny surface of my silver rucksack.

'It's my hot Latin blood!' I shouted back to him.

'Na—it's your hair gel,' Jimmi yelled after me.

The flies wouldn't leave me and I made for the tree-ring as fast as I could, the dirty little insects buzzing around my ears the whole time. I leapt into the circle and ran to the centre falling down laughing amidst the dried tail-end of summer leaves.

I waited for Jimmi with my eyes skyward. I watched the little patches of blue through the towering trees. I was spun out by the simplicity of the scene, the childish beauty of it.

'It's magical isn't it?' I said quietly, 'like being four years old again. The trees look so tall, so unreal.'

Jimmi didn't speak and when I looked up he was examining the bark of one of the pine trees, walking round and round it, checking at different heights.

'We used to mark them, me and my Mum,' he said, 'push coins in and that, so we knew when we came again.'

His voice was full of memories.

'It must be dreadful,' I said then, 'missing someone that much and not being able to talk to them or see them.'

Jimmi didn't reply. He just kept looking at the bark. I closed my eyes and felt the cool breeze against my face. The flies had gone so that was something.

'She used to say, 'Make a wish Jimmi,' and I'd stand right in the centre of the trees, with my eyes scrunched shut, my hands over them for extra measure, and I'd wish and wish so hard. She always asked what I wished for and I'd say, 'Not telling, it's a secret,' and run off. She used to try and catch me, she was so fast, so alive... You weren't meant to tell, she was a grown up, she should have known that.'

I got up out of the leaves and walked across to Jimmi. I stood behind him and slipped my hands across his eyes.

'Wish now,' I whispered in the shadow of the trees.

He took my hands slowly and let them drop away into the brittle air.

'There's no point,' he said calmly, 'You can't bring the dead back.'

We walked back to the car in silence with only the buzz of the flies in the hot summer sun and the whir of the crickets in the bushes. The heat of the sun through the windscreen made me feel sleepy and I drifted away into dreams. We left Cholsbury behind and drove into Old Amersham and found a pub where we drank warm sticky lager and ate bad fish and chips. We were laughing at the eighties tape that crackled out of the naff stereo beneath the whoop of the fruit machines.

'You set this up, didn't you?' Jimmi said laughing.

'Yeah right,' I said, 'I wanted to take you down memory lane. They'll put Ultravox on next!'

Jimmi laughed and I went back to my chips. I stood to get the beers in and 'Dancing With Tears in my Eyes' came on. We cracked up then.

'You got this played for me on hospital radio, d'you remember?' Jimmi said still laughing.

'Oh yeah! I wanted that other one, oh you know, the one we both liked.'

'Shit, what was it called?' Jimmi was screwing his face up trying to remember the track.

'D'you ever listen to them now?' I asked.

'Na,' he said, 'they're all on vinyl, I never got round to getting them on CD. Johnny's getting decks though, so maybe I'll give 'em a spin.'

'Probably sound shite now anyway!' I said, picking up our glasses and heading for the bar.

When I got back Jimmi was singing along to our adolescent favourite, 'Lament.'

I put his beer down in front of him and sat down.

'See, I requested the whole album,' I said.

'Nice touch babe.'

We swallowed our beer and listened to the music. Jimmi was ripping the label off his bottle of Bud and I was chain smoking my way through forty Marlboro. It was comfortable enough and I had no desire to rush back to London the way I usually did when I came home.

'Thanks,' Jimmi said quickly.

'What for?' I asked.

'For today—for being with me, taking my mind off things. I know it's a hassle for you, coming down from London and that.'

'Funny isn't it?' I said then, 'me spending your Mum's birthday with you when she never really liked me.'

'She didn't not like you, she didn't know you.'

'I know but I always felt odd around her, in the hospital and that,' I said.

It was strange, I could say anything to Jimmi, even stuff like that on a day like this one.

'She was just concerned. I don't think she understood us,' Jimmi said.

'I didn't understand us!' I answered, laughing.

'No,' he said sounding wistful.

I'd known Jimmi since I was twelve. I spotted him in a crowd of boys, hunched round a plastic table, drinking strawberry milkshake in Woolies caff. He stood out because of his hair. I used to call him 'the boy with bleached hair' to my mates but it wasn't bleached in those days, just sun kissed after a summer spent abroad. Spiky white blond against the cool grey green of his eyes. He had this crazy smile that lit his whole face up and crinkled the corners of his pretty eyes.

I used to live for Saturdays then. I remember the feeling of excitement that danced in my stomach on a Saturday morning. I would get the bus from Tring and parade around Aylesbury's naff shopping centre, dragging my school friends where I wanted to go. Looking for him. Following him around. Waiting alone in the caff for him to come in with his mates. Making a coffee last two hours like the girls did in Blue Jeans or Jackie. In my magazines the boy always noticed the girl sitting alone drinking coffee and thought she was mysterious or interesting. He would slip into the seat across from her and she would look up into his deep, sexy eyes and he'd say something like, 'Is this seat taken?' or 'Mind if I join you?'

Jimmi never said any of those things. One of his mates threw an empty crisp packet at me and they all laughed.

I got a friend to invite him to a party I was going to in Aston Clinton. He turned up with his mate Luke Wallace in tow as usual. I was wearing a pink miniskirt and an off the shoulder black top. I was thirteen and I felt dead grown up. I walked across to him and took his hand, then I led him upstairs and pulled him into what I thought was the spare room but was actually a junk room. When I pulled him down to the floor I cut my hand on some invisible metal object. It was pitch black in there and we groped around on the floor for ages, kissing and touching.

I gave him a blow job, my first ever I think but I didn't swallow. Then we went downstairs and he left with his mate and I went to get some cider and black. This girl from school came up to me then and started laughing. 'What's that?' she asked pointing at my T-shirt. 'What?' I asked looking down. Then everyone fell about laughing and I ran out mortified. It was right round town the next day, Jimmi Kemp came all over Jay Rossi's T-shirt! I cut a bit of it off and stuck it in my diary!

Jimmi and I didn't speak for ages after that, we were too embarrassed I suppose. Then he had this terrible motorbike accident. A friend called and told me. I went straight to the hospital. I was terrified of seeing him. I thought he might hate me. I stood by his bed and waited for him to wake up. He opened his eyes slowly and said, 'Bloody hell, Jay, what are you doing here?'

I went every day after that, 4.30PM, soon as school had finished, and I stayed until six most days.

I took Jimmi magazines or books to read, tapes I made at home of Ultravox, and dry shampoo so he could clean his hair. Every time I smell hospitals I think of those six months Jimmi was in hospital. Sometimes I'd go in and there'd be two or three other girls sitting around the bed flirting with him or Sandra his ex, running her perfectly manicured fuchsia nails up and down his arm, and we wouldn't be able to talk. When we were alone we talked a lot. We got close. I called him or he called me every night at 9PM sharp and we talked until my Dad shouted at me to get off the phone.

It shook me up, the thought of losing Jimmi. We still didn't get it together, though we talked about it a lot. I think he thought I was too young.

Then when I was fourteen I went to Tring Live Aid. I met this bloke who said he was in a band and before I knew it he was forcing himself into my tiny body, down an alley behind some houses. He was twenty one and I felt grown up. He turned out to be a total wanker, inviting me to stay the night with him having already arranged with his mates that I'd be there and 'up for it.' I left at three in the morning bruised and crying. I went to Jimmi. He made me tea and held me tight. So very tight. I don't remember being held before that night.

We got it together when I was seventeen and at art college. He was unemployed and living in the squat with Bo and some girlfriend. His live-in lover of the past two years.

Oh how it burnt me then.

We would snatch at precious seconds together, losing ourselves in the scent of our passion, the way it all was.

We wanted so much to talk but there was never time within the strength of our desire. Burning in our eyes like guilt. We wanted so much, so very much. The inaccessibility was enough. Then.

Then, then, then, the moments alone, the stolen seconds outside F.L.Y. Fully Liberate Yourself and believe me we did. Me, sucking on the top of his beer bottle only to be interrupted by her. And oh how he'd jump. Run away from those intimate moments of pleasure. Then he would go back to her. Her with her security. Her with her jealousy and paranoia. He never wanted any of it really, he wanted only to lie with me with my endless drug induced talk and deep on down, raw and ready sexing. And the way I was his equivalent, the female version of him. The way we were brother and sister. He wanted that so much more.

And then one day he came to me in the rain. Stood outside my window. I stole him in like a changeling. Took him into my arms and my bed and made him mine. He never looked back. I always knew I was enough for him. More. I filled him up completely just as he did me. He was the closest thing to perfect I ever found—I just never knew it.

By midnight I was on the Archway Road and just a spit from Tufnell Park. I parked the car outside the flat on the main road and climbed the stairs fast.

'Clemmi,' I shouted as I let myself in, tripping on the doormat and wishing I hadn't drunk so much in the King's Arms.

I suppose I should have expected it really. The curtains were closed and the bed was a mess and Clemmi was gone. 'Fuck!' I shouted to Jarvis the goldfish on top of the telly. 'Fuck it!'

I considered calling the police for exactly seven seconds and then realised that it wasn't too good a plan considering my recent misdemeanours. I grabbed my jacket and a fleece and slammed the door behind me.

I knocked on the door across from mine but Fat Frank was obviously asleep and refusing to answer the door. I tried the flat downstairs but the Goth couple who rarely showed their faces in daylight were too busy screwing to hear my knocks and I knew

Mark from upstairs was on nightshift. I ran out onto the rain soaked streets and began my search.

I checked out the all night caff on the corner, asked the drunks by the tube and the prostitutes by the NK Convenience Store but none of them had any answers and at 4AM I gave up and returned to the bedsit. I was soaking wet and totally fucked off and Fat Frank was up early and playing his beloved Beautiful South records very loud while hoovering his tiny room. I banged on the wall but he just turned the music up and played 'Old Red Eyes Is Back' about twenty times in a row before switching to Van Morrisson's 'Brown Eyed Girl' which was a hell of an improvement even if I was going to hear it twenty times.

I tried to get a couple of hours sleep but it was hopeless. I was dead tired but Jimmi wouldn't get out of my head. Not even Pulp could soothe my racing mind and by seven I was back out on the streets looking for Clem. I'd fucked up big time and I knew it. I bring the girl to England, dump her in my room and disappear for twelve hours. She was bound to be pissed off.

When the phone rang I grabbed it as fast as I could from under the pile of clothes in the corner. 'Clemmi?' I said quickly.

'No it isn't Jezebella, it is your mother.'

'Oh, hi mum.'

'What in the hell do you think you are doing? I have just had

Joanna on the phone in tears,' Mum sounded pretty upset. 'Where is Clemente?'

'Good question,' I answered.

'Now don't play games with me Jezebella.'

'Look, Mum, I don't know, I mean I did, she was here, but then I went down for Sasha's funeral and when I got back she'd gone.'

'Gone? Gone? What do you mean gone? What the hell were you doing in Italy anyway?'

'I went to get Clemmi, Mum,' I said making it sound simple.

'What in the hell for?' Mum said.

'Because I was worried about her.'

'Not too worried to leave her in London while you pop off to some junkie's funeral!'

'Sasha's my mate, I had to go, Jimmi was in a mess and..' I could hear the tears starting in my voice.

'I don't want any more of your silly little excuses. Now I am telling you my girl, you find your cousin and you drive her down here and then I'm putting her on the first flight back to Italy.'

'You can't do that Mum, she don't wanna be there.'

'Want to, Jezebella, want to,' Mum said in that irritating correctional tone I despised.

'But Mum...?' I tried.

'Your cousin is seriously ill, if she doesn't get her medication then who knows what she'll do. Now you better find her by tonight, I mean it Jezebella. I will expect you both by six o'clock.'

The phone went dead and I felt like smashing it against the wall. What fucking medication anyway? I remembered the handful of pills she swallowed in the airport toilets. Mum made Clemmi sound like some kind of psychopath. That got me thinking a bit. I mean what if Clemmi really was screwy. I mean what kind of thing was she likely to do? I was pretty worried she might hurt herself so I decided I should call Joanna and find out what the hell was going on with Clemmi.

'Pronto.'

'Aunty Joanna? It's me, Jay, Jezebella.'

'What the hell have you done with my daughter you slut?' I didn't exactly expect Joanna to be thrilled to hear from me but I thought the use of the word 'slut' was potentially a little bit on the strong side.

'She's here, in London.'

'Put her on the phone now, this second!' Joanna sounded sober for the first time in her life.

'I can't do that Joanna, she's... she's gone out... for a walk.'

'By herself?'

'Well yes,' I said.

'You stupid girl, don't you realise how ill she is? She must not be left alone.'

'Why? Come on Aunty she's just a bit down at the...'

'Down? Down? She's crazy, she's out of her mind and London is the worst place for her.'

'Well I just thought it'd be a break for her, get her away from Naples and that, away from her problems.' Well. It was the truth. From what I'd seen on my brief visit, Joanna was hardly doing that great a job herself.

'You stupid girl! Her problems are in London. Fabrizio is in London! If she finds him she'll... God knows, you better find her before she finds Fabrizio, I have to call him, warn him. When you find her take her home and phone me immediately, alright?'

'Yes Aunty, of course I will, but what's the problem with Fabrizio?'

'Just get out there and find her Jezebella!'

The phone went dead for the second time and I was getting pretty scared. I mean, why was Clemmi so pissed off with her own brother. I decided to call Fab myself and get the whole story. I rummaged through some papers for my phone book and found his number in Hampstead. I hadn't said goodbye to Fabrizio at the funeral and I knew he'd be pissed off with me and I felt kind of nervous about it. I dialled ferociously and when the line was dead I guessed I'd misdialled, so I tried again. Nothing.

I dropped the phone and pulled on my still damp jacket and headed for the outside world. I caught sight of my face in the mirror and I looked like shit. My eyes were red with huge shadows sitting beneath them. My mascara was smudgy and my eyelashes clogged together, my red stay-on-all-day lipstick a jammy faded mess after an hour of romping with Jimmi and walking the streets in the rain.

I searched my pockets for a wrap and found enough for a line. I snorted the gear quickly and ran down the stairs and jumped into the car, reaching through the open window to remove my fifth parking ticket of the week and chuck it into the glove compartment with the rest of the collection. I drove as fast as I could to Hampstead and pulled up outside Fabrizio's rather attractive split-level flat. I pushed on the buzzer for what seemed liked minutes and eventually a female voice said, 'Hello?'

'Hi, is Fabrizio there please?' I asked quickly.

'Fabrizio gone,' came the reply.

'Gone where?' I shouted, 'Has he moved out?'

'Yes, out, gone.'

'Where to?'

'He gone.' By now I was getting just a little bit frustrated.

'Where? Where has he gone?'

'Don't speak English good. No understand.'

Guessing she was Italian by her accent I tried again, in Italian.
'Aahh? Italiano?' came a friendlier response.
'Si, si. Eh Fabrizio?'
'Sta a Camden Town. Via Camden, numero tredici.'
'Grazie,' I said, *'Grazie tanto!'*
I guessed that Fab had been up to his old tricks and this girlfriend of his had kicked him out. I ran back to the car and headed for the Camden Road, scouring every door for number 13. When I found the blue chipped door I couldn't believe Fabrizio could be staying there however temporary the arrangement. It was a block of cheap bedsits and that definitely wasn't Fab's style. I hammered on the door. If anyone was in that dingy place they weren't planning on answering any doors. I decided my options were few and that I had little choice other than to sit on the dirty steps with their smell of putrid fish and piss, and wait till Fab got home.

I must have fallen asleep or something, because the next thing I knew some massive black boot was kicking me and I heard a voice shouting, 'Get the fuck away from my door girlie, howay.' I looked up into the face of the devil, some big geezer with orange dreadlocks and very few teeth. 'Hi,' I said rubbing my eyes. 'Never mind 'hi' lassie, get the fuck away from my front door,' said the bloke in a thick Geordie accent.

'Does Fabrizio live here?' I asked.

'Depends who's asking,' he said. Oh very bright.

'I'm his cousin, Jay,' I said.

'Never heard him tok about no cousin man,' said Geordie.

'Look when's he getting back?' I asked, getting impatient.

'He's na.'

'What?' I asked.

'He's away man.'

'Away where?'

'Away. Gone like,' said Geordie opening the door.

'Where?' I shouted getting really pissed off.

'Don't you shout at me, now howay ya micey cunt.'

'Look, it's important, family stuff. I need to know where he is'

Geordie looked up towards the sky then and gestured to the clouds above. 'Away,' he said, 'far away.' With those words he stepped into his hallway and before I could speak the door slammed in my face spitting flaky blue paint at my open mouth.

11. The Carnal Knowledge of Notting Hill Gate

I was fucked off big time. Geordie obviously wasn't all there. I went back to the flat and waited. What else could I do? I played Frente and Joni Mitchell and wondered what to do next. The doorbell rang suddenly in the darkness and I hoped to God it was Clemmi. I got up from my bed and I ran.

No Clemmi.

'Can I come in?'

'Yes,' I say because I need the flesh.

I need the feeling of warmth against my shaking body. I am so tired but I cannot bear to be alone and I cannot believe he is here today. I'd given him the chance to run after me and he didn't. But now he is here and I cannot ask him to leave. I cannot.

I open the door and he comes in. He touches my breast before he does anything else and I know I should know better but I don't. He touches me and I fall in. In to the deep blue cold warm thing he is and there it is, his hair, white gold on my dark skin, and the deep sea swell of his green eyes and I can see nothing but him. Nothing but his beauty and I want it. I want it hard and fast and soft and slow though he could never know. He could never know.

Take me somewhere sunny where there is nothing but me and you. Forget it all and love me. Please? I need love now in this empty space. Everything has left. Nothing safe sits here. I want to feel you inside me. I want to make you only mine. I am not scared of you being intimate with others. I am only scared that you will forget the way I feel. You don't know what it is to feel the way a woman feels. When I take a man inside me it is so fucking intimate. Don't you know how intimate it is. Don't you?

He slips into my flat and into my body as if it is home. I can't quite believe he's here. Every time I think of you I burn. Every time I touch you I want to cry. Do you know that you have the remote in your hands and that I am losing all control?

I cling to Jimmi and shake. With my ear tight to his chest I count the BPM's of his heart. And for once he is quiet. No jokes, no movements. All is still but for my shaking. All is perfectly silent. I know any second he will move away and reach for the cigarettes or go for a glass of water and I don't want the moment to pass. I want to stay in this statuesque silence.

'Jay?' Jimmi spoke so softly, 'are you OK?' He reached out his hand and smoothed my hair.

'What is it Jay?'

I wasn't sure I could manage an answer so I shrugged and clung tighter to his tight flesh and enjoyed the warmth of human contact. I wanted to say, 'I stabbed someone Jimmi. He's probably going to die.' Filthy words and I couldn't speak them.

We stayed there for a few minutes, with Jimmi stroking my hair until the shaking left my body and sleep came. When I woke Jimmi was watching me and smiled as I opened my eyes. 'I've missed you Jay. It's been so good, having you around again.' Jimmi looked sad and I knew how he felt. 'I was gutted when you left Jay, gutted.'

I kissed his nose and grinned. Then I remembered Clemmi and leapt from the bed to grab my combats and my T-shirt.

'Shit,' I yelled, 'what time is it? How long have we been asleep?' I looked for the alarm clock and found it by the phone which I'd left off the hook, which was possibly a good thing as Mum and Joanna had probably tried to call at least twenty times each. 'I've got to find Clemente,' I said.

'Where's she gone?' Jimmi asked, cigarette between his teeth.

'If I knew that, mate, I wouldn't be in big fucking trouble. Come on, get dressed.'

I filled Jimmi in on the mess I had made on the way to Camden Road. I had to ask this Geordie geezer what he meant by 'gone'; it was the only thread I had.

'So what's her problem with Fab?' Jimmi asked.

'God knows. I keep trying to work it out. They were always so close those two. I mean Clem being so angry with Fab, it don't make any sense at all.'

Jimmi switched the radio on and rummaged through the fag packets and parking tickets under his seat for a cassette. 'It must have been something real bad,' he said, 'something terrible.'

'Did Bo turn up?' I asked.

'Na, Ziggy's still looking I imagine.'

'Jesus, we should open a missing person's bureau!' I said. We pulled up outside the house and Jimmi jumped out the car and hammered on the door.

'Sorry Jay,' he said, 'but I can't imagine Fab in a place like this, no way man, you know what he's like.'

'Well I did,' I answered, 'but to tell you the truth he was a bit odd at the funeral, anyway, shit happens.'

The door opened then and a girl of about fifteen stood there, smoking a cigarette. She was thin and pretty in a sort of adolescent model way. Her hair was in bunches and she was wearing a man's shirt and not much else.

'Yeah?' she said looking at me with wide blue eyes.

'I'm looking for Fabrizio,' I said, trying not to sound as frantic as I felt.

'Fabi?' she asked.

'Yes,' I said quickly, 'he's my cousin'

'He went out,' she said, 'with his sister.'

'Clemmi?' I asked.

'Yeah, something like that, small girl, dark hair.' She took a drag on her cigarette and leant against the door frame.

'Was she OK?' I asked, 'was Fabi OK?'

'Oh yeah,' she said, 'he was really pleased to see her, didn't even know she was in the country.'

'Do you know where they went?' I asked, thrilled that this girl was being so helpful and that Geordie hadn't got to the door first.

'Said something about a place in Notting Hill, a restaurant they used to go to.'

'Luciano's?' I asked quickly.

'Something like that. His sister wanted to show him something there. He said they wouldn't be long though, we're meant to be going out tonight.'

Jimmi and I simultaneously sprinted back to the car and I wondered what Fabrizio was doing with this kid.

'If you find him, tell him not to be late,' she shouted, but we were already pulling away.

'Fab's obviously not pissed at Clemente or he wouldn't have gone with her,' Jimmi said.

'Who knows? Fucking traffic, it's gonna take us ages to get to Notting Hill.'

'Cut through the city,' Jimmi suggested.

'Yeah right, like you know!' I said.

Luciano was an old family friend. Clemmi, Fab and me had spent hours at his restaurant as kids, playing under the tables or with the plastic coin fountain in the corner while our parents got pissed on *grappa*. Uncle Claudio and my Dad knew Luciano from way back, from Palermo, and the restaurant was a regular hangout despite the distance.

Renato, the chef, used to make us *Gelato al Limone* in half lemons with cocoa powder on top. He got me a present once. The Italian national outfit: a little black dress with flowers on and a white apron that went over the skirt. I wore it with my hair in plaits and he'd call me *La Principessa*. That was before Joanna and Claudio decided to go to Italy to escape the tax bills and their marital misdemeanours. Fabrizio had come back to England the minute he was sixteen. He hated Italy. But Clemmi, being younger, settled down there and ended up staying.

'*Gelato al Limone* for three,' Renato said grinning at us from under his moustache.

'*Grazie tanto*,' we all said in unison.

'*Prego ragazzi, prego.*'

Mummy was drinking Sambucca and smoking Italian cigarettes. Joanna was shouting at Claudio and we all knew she'd had too much to drink. Even at the age of ten I knew Joanna was an alcoholic. Clemmi was eating her ice-cream and Fabrizio, who was much taller than us, said,

'I know something you don't know!'

'What?' Clemmi asked, her mouth full and chocolate powder all over her chin.

'Something secret,' Fab said.

'Tell us,' I said, poking Fab's ribs.

'Mum's got a boyfriend!'

'Don't be silly,' I said, 'she's married to uncle Claudio.'

'I heard Dad tell her off about her boyfriend. And he called her a *puttana* and said, "We're going back to Italy if it doesn't stop." I heard him.'

Clemmi didn't seem to understand but I remember looking at Aunty Joanna and feeling horrible.

'And I heard Dad say it's been going on for years, since before Mum had Clemmi.'

'Shut up Fabi that's not true,' Clemmi said. 'Mummy loves Papa.'

Fabrizio didn't say any more but they left for Italy a few weeks later after a lot of shouting and a lot of Clemmi and Fabi staying the night at our house. They would have gone to Palermo, where the family was from, but Claudio had messed up some family business and couldn't go back there, so they ended up in Naples.

'Have you got 'This Is Hardcore'?' Jimmi asked me.

'Sorry?' I said, lost in memories.

'It's alright, I'm gonna put another Pulp tape on.'

'Which one?' I asked.

'Gotta guess!' said Jimmi playing the old game we used to play in the car on the way to outdoor parties back in the 80's. Name that tune. Guess it after one bar. Give up? Two bars? Intro. Got it. Yeah! Wicked. My turn. Let's do another? Over and over on those long journeys, the game broken only to tune into pirate radio stations for instructions or to stop at a garage to wait for our mates.

The music spun around the car.

'As the sign outside proclaimed, nature sometimes makes a mistake, is it the mother or the father to blame...'

'Um, *Anorexic Beauty* no, no, uh, got it, I've got it, *Freaks.*'

Jimmi turned the stereo up. 'No, track title not album title please.'

'Umm?'

'Give up?' Jimmi asked sounding pleased.

'No, 'nother two bars,' I said, determined to get it.

'Want a clue?' Jimmi asked as impatient as ever.

'No,' I said emphatically, 'uh, *Fairground.*'

'Got it in... far too many!'

The music screamed from the tinny car stereo and I turned my thoughts over. Why did Clemmi want to go back to Luciano's? It had closed down when Luciano had gone on the run from some Sicilians he owed money to; it was probably a Chinese Takeaway these days. What the fuck did she want with taking Fabrizio there? I mean if she wanted to have things out with him why not do it where she found him? As soon as she found him.

We parked up near the Portobello Road and walked past the cinema towards where Luciano's used to be. I hardly recognised the street. I hadn't been there for years and the row of shops beside it was all different. Amazingly, the restaurant was still there; it was boarded up, but it was still there and the front window still had the Tricolore painted above it.

'It's closed down. What now?' Jimmi said.

'Come on, let's try and get in.'

'What for Jay, they've probably gone somewhere else for dinner.'

'Somehow Jimmi,' I said, 'I don't think Clemmi's got dinner in mind.'

We walked round the back until we found the alley that ran down behind the shops. Jimmi was singing a song off the compilation tape and as much as I love Pulp for some reason it irritated me, the words irritated me.

'Little girl with blue eyes there's a hole in your heart, and one between your legs, Never had to wonder which one he's gonna fill in spite of what he said...'

I jumped over the gate and waited for Jimmi, then scanned the row of yards to see which was Luciano's. I recognised the mock marble pillars that used to stand either side of the entrance lying smashed across each other in the back yard.

'That's it,' I said jumping the fence, 'Come on Jimbo.'

The back door was slightly ajar and I guessed Clemmi and Fab were already inside. I wondered how she'd managed to lure him to that dead place. I gestured to Jimmi to stay quiet and slipped into the dark and dusty restaurant, my old playground.

Inside it was so dark I could barely see a thing. Jimmi was close behind me and I was glad he was there. Faint voices were coming from the kitchens; I crept towards them and recognised Clemmi's voice. I whispered to Jimmi to stay back.

In the light that fell from the streetlamp outside, I could see Fabrizio sitting by the old larder, his hands behind his back, his face like death. This wasn't the clean cut yuppie I recalled from the funeral: Fabi was thin and pale with the red pinned eyes of a smackie and the gaunt stare of a madman. I wondered if the stuff at the funeral had been a show; the flash car, the big talk. What was he doing living in a bedsit on Camden Road with a girl young enough to be his daughter?

'This is ridiculous Clemmi,' Fabrizio was saying.

'Shut up *bastardo!* I want you to tell me the truth.' Clemmi gestured as she spoke and I saw the glint of a knife in her hand. My knife in her hand. The hunting knife Felty gave me for Christmas last year. I thought maybe Fabi's hands were tied up but I couldn't be sure.

'I am, now put the knife down.'

Fab saw me then but Clemmi was unaware, I was behind her.

'You were fifteen years old. I was six Fabrizio. You were my brother. *Tu sei mio fratello!*'

Clemmi was crying, nearly hysterical. 'How could you do it Fab? *Come hai potuto fare una cosa del genere?*'

'I didn't do it Clemmi. I love you. I wouldn't hurt you ever.'

'*Perche Fabrizio? Ti volevo bene.*'

'I didn't do it. Please Jay, make her stop?'

Clemmi spun round and saw me by the door.

'Oh just like the old days!' she shouted, her voice twisting horribly, 'Just the three of us in the kitchen at Luciano's.'

'Put the knife down Clemmi,' I said.

'You saw it all Jay, didn't you, tell him you saw him do that to me. You were there, standing right there by the door weren't you Jezzy? I saw you. You were just standing there and Mum and Dad were drinking *Tia Maria* that night and we had *Gelato al Limone*. *Me lo ricordo*. And we went into the larder and... he raped me and you saw it all. I'm not crazy, I'm not. I remember it all now.

All of it.'

Clemente moved suddenly towards Fabrizio with the knife.

'You've ruined my life you bastard.'

'No Clemmi, stop it!' I said grabbing at her wrist but she darted out of the way and turned the knife on me.

'You saw him do it and you never said anything.' Clemmi was manic, shouting and crying.

'You let them take me away to Italy after he did that to me. And I blocked it out Jezzy, because it was so awful. But it came back. They made it come back. *Non sono pazza. Me lo riccordo.*'

'You've got it wrong Clem,' Fabrizio said, 'I never hurt you.'

'But I remember it,' Clemente screamed, 'I'm not going mad, I'm not. *Me lo riccordo.*'

It all began to make sense to me. The psychiatrist and Joanna thinking she'd gone mad, and Clemmi's memory. Jesus Christ what a mess. Clemmi looked wild. Her pupils were dilated and her hair was ragged. She gripped the knife tight in both her hands and I knew she was serious.

'This is ridiculous Clemente,' Fabrizio shouted walking towards us and the door. 'I'm getting out of here.'

'No,' Clemente screamed, 'No.'

Aiming the knife at his throat Clemmi ran towards Fabrizio and time stood still. Jimmi came out of nowhere, seizing her wrist as the knife met Fabrizio's skin. It pierced the space between his throat and chest. And I watched it sink into his flesh. Straight away blood began to spurt from the wound, and Fabrizio made horrific gurgling sounds as he fell to the floor. Jimmi was holding Clemmi who was shaking and screaming.

I ran to Fabrizio not knowing what to do, my mind taken over by the man on the bed in King's Cross.

'Call an ambulance Jimmi,' I shouted.

Everything was blurry and fast and slow at the same time and I didn't really have a clue what was going on. When the ambulance came I was pushed away from Fabrizio's bleeding body. Jimmi sat in the corner of the room holding on to Clemmi who was staring into space like the nutter they all thought she was.

I sat with Clemente in the back of the police car and held her hand. I realised my own danger in the presence of the police but I guess I was past caring. Recognition would almost be a relief. I squeezed Clemmi's hand and said,

'He didn't do it Clemmi. Not to you.'

'I'm not mad,' she repeated.

'No you're not,' I said, 'you're not mad.'

I watched the houses and trees and cars and people that we passed. Everything normal, usual, the same grey city. The same vacant stares on pallid faces. The rush. The rush and surge of the

pedestrians pouring from the tube stations. Scavenging on the
flesh of the city, spreading their filth and dirt and disgust. I sat
with Clemmi in our chauffeur driven cage and let it all pass. I was
thinking of the man in the hotel room. His sweat and stench, his
hairy shoulders and the rolls of fat around his waist, his terrified
stare as the knife sank in to his flabby white chest with its spider
leg hairs. I thought of Fabrizio, screaming and bleeding and
maybe dead. Maybe dead.

'Come on Fabi let's play in the kitchen.'

'We can't, Clemmi's too young, she's not allowed in the kitchen.'

'Let's leave her here then. Come on.'

Fabi and I waited until Clemmi went to the loo and all the
adults were busy chatting, and we darted off towards the kitchens
giggling. The restaurant was closed, Luciano and Renato were
sitting chatting to Papa and Mum, Guilio the kitchen porter had
left ten minutes before and Joanna and Claudio were arguing.

'This way,' Fabi whispered, gesturing to the larder. I began to
giggle again and Fabi put his hand over my mouth. 'Ssshhh,' he
said. 'Now let's play our favourite game.'

I felt the funny feeling between my legs when he said it. 'OK,' I
said, lying down on the larder floor.

'Take your knickers off then Jezzy.'

I hitched up my skirt and took my knickers off. Fabi began to touch between my legs and rub me where I liked it. He didn't do it for very long before he said, 'My turn,' undoing his trousers. He got his thingy out and put my hand on it. 'Rub it harder,' he said, 'and faster.' I rubbed his erect penis the way he had showed me so many times before.

'Harder Jezzy,' he said, 'do it harder and faster.' He guided my small hand, 'Faster, harder and faster.'

'It's getting bigger,' I said giggling.

'That's because it likes you,' Fabi said. 'Do you want me to put it inside you?'

'Where?' I said. I didn't know what Fabi meant.

'In there,' he said touching me between my legs again.

'OK,' I said.

Fabi showed me how to lie down with my legs open and he spat on his fingers to make them wet and then rubbed me again. It felt nice but funny, not like before, not like the game. He was breathing heavily and fiddling with his thing, trying to put it in me.

'Are you sure that's where it goes?' I said.

'Yes,' said Fabi, 'I saw Mum do it with her boyfriend.'

'When?' I asked.

'On Monday when Dad was at work and I came home from school early with flu.' Fabi managed to get it inside me a bit.

'Ouch!' I said, 'It hurts Fabi.'

Fab didn't seem to hear me. He was trying to push it all the way in and the pain was getting worse and worse. I gave a little yelp and Fabi pushed his hand across my mouth so I couldn't make any noise. He started pushing it in and out of me and it hurt so much I thought I'd faint. I tried to tell him to stop but his hand was pushing down on my mouth, harder and harder as he pushed himself inside me. Pain shot through me with every thrust. It went on for ages and I was crying and his breathing was really heavy and his face looked horrid and then I heard a terrible scream.

Fabi stopped and collapsed on top of me and that was when I saw her. Clemmi was standing by the larder door crying.

'You're not going crazy Clemmi. It was you at the door,' I said. 'It was me in there with Fabrizio. It was me he did that to.'

Clemmi's eyes began to focus. The messed up, shattered memories were finally falling into place.

'You?' she said.

'Yes,' I answered softly. 'Just before you all left for Italy.' Looking down at my hands I wished I'd never had to tell her. Wished I'd never remembered our horrible secret game.

'Oh God,' Clemmi said leaning back against the seat.

'He'll be alright, Clem, I'm sure it didn't go that deep. It probably looked worse than it was.' I spoke with the knowledge of someone who had driven a knife into flesh.

I hugged Clemente to me, secretly respecting her bravery when all I'd been left with for years was silence and the bitter crust that had formed around my heart, and my mistrust of men. Use them and abuse them before they do it to you. Treat them mean, keep them keen, then fuck their heads. Not break their hearts as much as rip them out and grind them into the ground. No emotion. Don't let it show. Keep it in.

Do shitloads of drugs to fill the gap. Sleep with strangers. Sleep with friends. Friends of friends. Anyone I can get my hands on. Love 'em and leave 'em, kick them when they're down. Run away before you get in deep or you might fall in love. A catalogue of hate and destruction. Trust no-one, not even myself. A trip up lonely street to the club of no regrets. I regret nothing.

I could have written the S.C.U.M manifesto; I live it, that's for sure. I'm not sorry for knifing that bastard and no court will make me say that I am. I knew what I was doing. I may not have much of a heart left but I do love you. You were the only one I ever loved. Safe in our drugged up bliss. Just us. Loving it all. Jesus, Jimmi we were so loved up. We were

so
loved
up.

12. Irrelevant Pinchcock and the Breadboard Junkies

Jimmi and I sat in the Maynard drinking double vodkas and taking in the warmth of the summer evening. They'd done the pub up a bit. Extended it.

They'd ditched the old bowling alley in favour of extending the seating area. The staff wore new t-shirts, bright red with The Maynard Arms emblazoned across the chest. The decor hadn't changed much. The fishing memorabilia was still there. I noticed that the carp had been moved to the back of the pub and some new signs had gone up. Sort of mock old fashioned signposts, declaring that Manchester was 410 miles one way and apparently we were only 2 miles south of Inverness. Some dickhead had shoved a sign promising Newcastle 110 right in front of the sports screen and a geezer in an Arsenal shirt was protesting loudly about the view.

Jimmi had gone back to Tring after the drama at Luciano's and I was too scared to ask if it was permanent. I was keeping my distance in the aftermath of our recent encounters. I swallowed the last of the vodka and lit a cigarette inhaling deeply.

'How's Fabrizio?' Jimmi asked.

'Better,' I said. 'They reckon he'll be out by next week.'

'What about Clem?' Jimmi said sucking his ice cubes.

'She's staying with my Mum and Dad for a bit. Until she's feeling better. Fabi covered up, said it was an accident and that.'

'Did the rozzers believe it?'

'Probably,' I said, 'most of them are as thick as shit! Anyway, it's a domestic and if Fab doesn't want to press charges there's nothing they can do.'

I thought about going out into the garden to skin up, but the sound of those stupid caged birds tweeting loudly came through the open door and I dropped the idea.

'Ziggy found Bo,' Jimmi said.

'Yeah, where was he?' I asked genuinely concerned.

'On a Buddhist retreat in Swindon. Trying to block it all out I guess.'

'Right.' I felt kind of uneasy.

'Ziggy and Bo want to move up, maybe Johnny too.'

'Yeah, yeah,' I said sarcastically, 'like they did five years ago.'

'Na, seriously,' Jimmi said.

Irrelevant Pinchcock came in then and sat down at our table. I didn't bother doing introductions. It didn't seem worth it. Jimmi wasn't likely to stay around long.

'I've done it Jay,' Pinch said looking very proud.

'Done what mate?' I asked, not particularly bothered.

'I kicked out the smackies. Last night. Changed the locks and everything,' Pinch said proudly.

'Well done Pinch,' I said, feigning enthusiasm, 'good on yer.'

'Just got to find four new lodgers now. Don't know anyone looking do yer? I mean I don't wanna advertise because I might get more smackies and then I'll be back to square one, trade four smackies for four more smackies.'

'No, sorry mate,' I said.

Jimmi jabbed me in the ribs,

'I do,' he said, 'me and my mates is looking and so's Jay but we'll share a room.'

'Jimmi?' I said. 'Wanna discuss it with me first?'

'We could all move in tomorrow mate. Jay your place is crap, too fuckin' small for both of us. Yeah we'll take it. It'll be good for all of us, a new start.'

'Great,' Pinch said, 'none of them are smackies are they?'

'No,' said Jimmi.

'Alright then, it's a deal,' Pinch said.

'Wicked man, I'll call them now.'

'Seems a nice bloke,' Pinch said as Jimmi went to call the others.

I watched him standing by the phone trying to get the money into the slot failing miserably and ruffling his funny hair.

'Yeah, he is,' I said slowly, 'he's alright is Jimmi.'

I felt secretly pleased about him wanting to live with me and a change of address would certainly keep the heat off.

'Looks like we're gonna be flatmates then Jay?'

'Yeah, looks like it. Hey Pinch, maybe it's time for you to tell me your real name, if we're gonna be flatmates and that, I mean I'll see it on the post anyway won't I?'

'I've told you before Jay,' Pinch said lifting his pint and winking at me, 'it's Irrelevant.'

I laughed loud and we clinked our glasses. Jimmi was chattering away on the phone and he turned to smile at me. I smiled back, feeling warm.

The door to the pub swung open.

The smile slipped from my lips.

Genie was in the doorway, her face pale.

I stood slowly and made my way across the pub. Jimmi blew me a kiss as I passed and stuck his tongue out playfully.

Genie stood facing me. Her eyes were wide and frightened. She spoke slowly as if trying to understand what she was saying.

'They're on to us Jay. The police. They've been asking questions. They were here, last night, looking for us. He's dead Jay. We have to get out.'

I looked across at Jimmi as he put the phone down. I watched him walk over to Pinch and ask something. His eyes scanned the pub for me.

I followed Genie out of the door slowly, knowing what we had
to do. I heard Jimmi call my name from across the crowded bar.
We left the pub door swinging against the night. I saw the car
parked across the road, a shiny red Alpha Romeo Spider
convertible with cool chrome bumpers and warm leather seats. It
had the speed we required.

I didn't look back.

Emilia di Girolamo was born in 1971 and raised in
Buckinghamshire. She gained a First in Drama at
Middlesex University and is currently writing up a PhD
on drama with offenders. Emilia has worked extensively
in prisons and with probation clients as well as lecturing
in creative writing at Middlesex University. In 1997 her
play '1000 Fine Lines' received critical acclaim for its
London run. Emilia has previously had short fiction
published in 'The Printers Devil' and 'London Magazine.'
Emilia di Girolamo now lives in Crouch End.

di Girolamo is a crafty story teller / Time Out